Ascension — Before Stars

Book I — Highspire Academy | The Observers | The Sacred Invention

by J. Markavian

First Edition

2025

Paperback ISBN: 978-1-918005-01-1
Hardback ISBN: 978-1-918005-21-9
EBook ISBN: 978-1-918005-41-7

Illustrations by John Beech
Cover design by mkv25.net/books

For sales and permissions, contact: books@mkv25.net

Discover more books and digital editions at: jmarkavian.com

First Edition, 2025

Printed in the United Kingdom.

Ascension — Before Stars

Prologue — In the Vault

In a distant age, within the crystal-lit vaults of the Ascendant Archives, aged fingers paused on the letters of a long-treasured memory. The record had been carefully preserved, cross-referenced from different sources, and engraved deep below the dais where the pages sat.

Through silent lips, the memory read as follows:

> *The first snow fell softly across the tower's twisted stones.*
>
> *We met in silence. They spoke in glyphs.*
>
> *The spiral was never drawn the same way twice.*
>
> *It always began with her mark, and ended with his.*
>
> *We never spoke of love—yet the stars remember for them, even now.*

The vault light shimmered. The page turned without sound. The moment replayed.

Somewhere below, across a small town in the valley, the snow began to fall again.

Part I — Highspire Academy

Chapter I — The Boy in the Tower

Year 2000, Lantern Light, 18th day — Music spilled through the arches; no player could be found.

Highspire Academy smelled brightly of dust, paper, and distant rain. The base of the academy was a place older than maps could properly frame. Carved into a ridgeline overlooking a wide valley with a sleepy town below, it wasn't built for comfort, though it offered it nonetheless. The stone halls held a quiet that clung to students' robes like frost on branches. Magic was rarely taught here through spark or wand—but by repetition, translation, and theory. Magic lived in the margins, in spaces between diagrams, in sleepless nights and hushed conversations.

Helena smoothed the wrinkles from her skirt as she stepped through Highspire's arches. Her mother had fretted over her bag, but everything had been packed days before. What occupied her instead were the glyph circuits carved into the stonework—reminders that the kingdom's power ran on patterns she was only just beginning to decipher.

Highspire attracted the best of Wynnal—unlicensed mages who proved their skill and acumen. The Kingdom's magic was old: glyph-circuits carved into stone and soil, channelled through leylines to power cities and guard its borders. Helena had passed test after test, each one more intricate than the last. She was naturally gifted, yes—but also examined, vetted, and recommended, until Highspire itself became the only path forward.

Life after school meant a ministry post, or a guild position— wherever her skills found demand.

Later that afternoon, after bag drop and introductions, she explored the east wing alone—her footsteps muffled by ancient carpet and polished stone. Her black uniform, freshly pressed, hung loosely with sleeves a little too long for her arms. She tugged her satchel tighter against her shoulder, heavy with unopened books and a tin of salted almonds—her mother's insistence. She stared wide-eyed as high ceilings soared overhead, carved with blocky runes and flowing glyphworks.

She was fourteen, sharp-eyed and stubborn. A girl who read too fast and trusted too slowly. Not a girl keen to be noticed, or concern herself with others—but already she had heard his name at lunch.

> *"Aurelian," whispered over tea.*
> *"A prefect in the west wing," said a fourth-year, wide-eyed.*

> *"Never attends class—but aces every test," murmured another.*
>
> *"Just heed what he says," someone warned.*
>
> *"You won't find him wandering the halls, but he reports everything we do to the staff."*

Helena hadn't responded. She had only written the name in the corner of her notes, without underlining it.

The first time she saw him, it was from across the courtyard —up in the tower window where the old star maps were stored. He sat half-shadowed, bent over a notebook. The late sun caught the curve of his cheek. He didn't look mysterious. He looked... tired. Quiet. Reserved. Like someone holding his breath to create a private space only he could feel.

That should have been the end of it.

But that evening, as she unpacked her things in the dormitory, she found a scrap of parchment tucked into the back of her notebook.

On it, in tiny precise lettering, was a single carefully copied glyph.

A spiral of three turns, each loop marked by a single dot of red ink.

She froze. Not out of fear—but recognition.

She had invented that symbol three months ago.

It wasn't part of any standard spell theory. She had doodled it in the margins of her journal, theorizing about cyclical patterns in enchantment flow, using fractal recursion to self-sustain a simple glyph. You couldn't find it in any book. She hadn't shown it to anyone.

How?

She turned the parchment over. It was blank.

She stared at the symbol for a long time; the dormitory around her filled with chatter, laughter, and the squeak of opening trunks. Someone played a lute in the hallway. Another dropped a jar.

Helena held the scrap like it might burn her. Time blurred, then rushed around her as the echoes grew, until she swept herself away from the moment to find her room.

Far above, in the west tower, the boy in the window closed his notebook—and stepped into shadow, just as the stars began to stir.

Chapter II — Shared Silence

Year 2000, Frostfall, 15th day — A disagreement became a vow.

Highspire Academy, Public Library, First Week of Term, After Dusk

The library door opened with a breath.

No creak nor clatter. The gentle sway pushed back by ten thousand books sleeping in shelves of old wood, and even older enchantment. The lights above were dim—crystal globes pulsing a soft glow across dew-covered moons, brightening in gentle rhythm with the footfall beneath them.

Helena stepped through the archway in fresh wool-soft slippers, a thin grey blanket around her shoulders like a cloak—her hair tied primly back, loose strands brushing her shoulders. It was well past dusk. She had told the dormitory girls she was tired. She was not.

Her silver-laced notebook sat tucked under one arm. Her glyph still burned in her mind—that spiral, those three red dots. A shape that had no business appearing in anyone else's handwriting. And yet... there it was. In perfect mirror of her own, even the ink bled the same.

She didn't believe in coincidence.

Not here. Not now.

She came to find a silence she could speak inside.

The public study floor was open—polished stone and oak tables lit by bristling spellflame, along neat orderly rows. Some students whispered at desks. A few dozed with ink-stained fingers—those who had tried, and failed, to work beyond their limits.

Helena moved to the far corner, where the windows looked out onto the frost-flecked gardens. She didn't need to find him. She wasn't even looking.

But he was already there.

He sat angled to the room, at the end of the far row, giving him the perfect vantage to observe movement in and out of the library. Beside him, books were stacked into three neat piles. They were not arranged by author or subject, but by age. Helena noticed that immediately. Ancient, worn volumes on the left. Fresh copies on the right. His own notes lay in the centre. As she approached, she sensed a whisper of words and meta glyphs flowing between them. In the dim light she could almost see connections forming from within the pages.

He didn't look up when she passed.

She didn't stop.

But she circled once after selecting a few curiosities from the shelves. Balancing her choices, she casually drifted back —slipping into the seat beside him.

Not across.

Not behind.

Beside.

He glanced at her directly. The kind of glance that wasn't rude, more... noting. He refocused forward.

She waited. Counted the seconds.

He turned his page, holding the paper lightly between his fingers for a thoughtful moment.

She opened her notebook.

An empty page, quill in hand. Briskly, she sketched a simple push glyph and wrote:

| *"You copied my spiral."*

The words quietly sounded across the space between them.

Not accusing. Not nervous. Just curious.

Aurelian didn't respond immediately. *Was she really using simple magic instead of speaking?* He reached for a pencil, underlined something twice, then closed his book with a quiet *thunk.*

> *"I didn't copy it," he said, in a low, certain tone. "I found it. In a field journal tucked behind the astronomy shelves."*

Helena looked up towards his hazel brown eyes, glinting gold in the spellflame, and blinked away a thought.

> *"That's where I left it," she whispered, recalling her fumble earlier in the day.*

A silence fell between them—not awkward, but intrigued.

Aurelian's gaze stayed steady on her quill hand. He studied her not like an enemy. Not like a boisterous crush. Like a theory. Like every fibre of her soul was being unravelled.

> *"Tell me, what were you trying to solve?"*

Helena hesitated. Then reached into her bag, pulled out the same journal, and opened to a page full of loops and arrows.

> *"Energy loss through spell decay," she uttered. "If you fold the cycle back on itself, and trace the path from origin to origin, the loop sustains just long enough to store... memory. A magical echo."*

Aurelian nodded curtly.

> *"Most intriguing."*

And then—he smiled. The slightest smile at the corner of his mouth.

> *"You left a note in the margin. 'This could be beautiful.'"*

The colour in Helena's cheeks rose faintly. Brushing the hair behind her ear with her spare hand, she lowered her head to hide a smile.

> *"It still might be."*

She guided him towards the back of her notebook, where she had penned pages of notes exploring all manner of possibilities.

They sat like that for a while.

The silence changed shape.

No longer empty.

Now full.

Not loud—full of warmth.

They read together. Shared notes. Scribbled suggestions.

And at some point—just as the library lights dimmed further to signal the final hour—Aurelian turned towards her and spoke without looking up:

> *"I return here every seventh night. After midnight. I study what I'm not taught in the curriculum. And where I can't find answers, I write, I experiment."*

Helena met his eyes.

> *"I'll bring better notes next time."*
>
> *"That would bring me joy," he said.*

And that was all.

They packed their books with a polite shyness, and parted at the door.

With a promise too joyful to forget—and a glance too delicate to break.

Chapter III — The Spark Beneath the Snow

Year 2000, First Snow, 1st day — The sky fell in silence

Crisp snow had fallen overnight, forming soft mounds deliberately across the landscape.

The white sheet dressed the academy's courtyards in silver hush, tucked frost into the crooks of stone benches, and softened every edge of Highspire's austere silhouette. The wind was still. The sky above was full of stars.

Helena's boots whispered over the path from the east dormitory, leaving narrow prints behind her—curving a single thread of memory across a page of white.

She hadn't intended to walk here this early. But the quiet called her.

Her slightly frayed woollen scarf trailed behind her coat. Her breath curled visibly in the air. There was no one else outside. Only the warm chattering of waking students, barely audible now, as she stepped further from the archway.

Except—she squinted—there~

Near the arch of the west wing dormitories. Aurelian.

He stood incautiously next to a frozen flowerbed, a short wooden staff in hand, its tip glowing faintly gold. His wrist moved slowly, deliberately, sketching a shape through the snow.

A curling sigil, personal to him. Wide, soft, and slow-turning. Three loops. She approached, silent.

He didn't look up. She didn't ask. She simply stood with him. Not across. Not behind. At his side.

Then, without a word, she crouched and pressed her gloved fingertip into the spiral's outer ring.

A single red dot appeared.

She stood again, brushing her hands together. Her eyes met his, just briefly.

> *"That's not how I would've closed it,"* Aurelian said *quietly.*
>
> *"I know," Helena replied. "But it's how it wants to close."*

A pause. The stafflight flickered.

> *"Maybe it does."*

They stood like that a while, snow softening the night around them. The silence grew—not tense, but expectant, as if something unseen was about to land.

Above, the stars hung low, cold and bright before the sunrise could fade the blanket of night.

"Do you ever wish the snow would stay?" she asked.

Aurelian didn't answer immediately.

"No," he said at last. "But I do wish we had longer to study between melts."

Helena turned her gaze back to the glyph.

"If time could bend," he murmured, "I'd study the same moment twice."

She smiled brightly to the floor.

"I think I already am."

Their hands brushed—not quite an accident, not quite on purpose. Her glove touched his bare fingers for only a second.

But that was enough.

Aurelian lowered his staff once more to draw a closing line—a gentle curve that met her red dot and sealed the spiral at her feet. The glyph pulsed a single time; a soft breath of light spreading across the snow, drifting through the footprints of the courtyard, gently sending a sparkling helix of snowflakes into the sky.

Part II — The Observers

Interlude — Echoes in the South Garden

Year 2000, Lantern Light, 6th day — Long shadows, wet flagstones

Students were gathered in the south garden courtyard as the sun fell into late afternoon. A rare window of free time before dusk classes. The leaves haven't started turning, but the shadows are growing longer, and the fountain began to splash sounds in falling glyphs again—barely audible, like a spell half-remembered.

Wynn had managed to swipe two sugar-dusted apple tarts from the lower dining hall. How? No one knew, but she'd done it smiling, and with a wink.

> *"If you eat yours too slow, I'm eating it too," she warned Helena, nudging her gently on the garden bench.*

Wynn rattled through her satchel searching for a familiar touch; buttons, stones, ticket stubs, a painted feather, a blue marble flecked with gold. A dozen or so tiny tokens, each carrying their own story.

Wrapped in her reading shawl, legs tucked under her— Helena took a neat bite and said nothing.

But the second bite was faster.

Across the path, Faye and Ariela had discovered a sun patch on the old mosaic steps and had taken to it like cats. Faye was attempting to sketch the lightplay off her friend's hair.

Ariela, predictably, was telling a story involving a broken compass, three river spirits, and a goat that may or may not have been enchanted.

> *"...and that's when I realised it wasn't a goat. It was the headmistress's familiar. In disguise."*
>
> *"You're making this up," Faye said, not looking up from her notebook.*
>
> *"Am I?" said Ariela defiantly.*
>
> *"Yes," replied Faye.*
>
> *"Only mostly."*

Faye allowed the smallest smile. Ariela grinned like she'd won something.

Near the fountain, Lyla was casting practice glyphs in the air—tight, sharp, controlled. Each stroke snapped into shape before vanishing an inch above the ground. She worked alone, steady and focused—until Wynn called across:

> *"You're going to rupture the aether if you keep bullying it like that."*
>
> *"Good," Lyla muttered. "Maybe then it'll finally listen."*

Helena smirked softly. Lyla didn't look, but her lip twitched.

Watching all of this, Aurelian stood at the far edge of the courtyard, his back to an archway, half-shadowed by creeping ivy. Hidden in plain sight. Observing not out of duty—but rhythm.

Aurelian witnessed.

Not as a prefect. Not as a supervisor.

As someone still deciding whether he belonged *near* them... or *with* them.

A student from another house approached—briefly pulling Aurelian out of reverie—to ask him about permissible glyphworks. He gave a brief answer: direct, polite, reassuring. Then returned his gaze to the group.

And then, as though waiting for the moment, Helena turned. Her eyes flicked toward him—not an invitation, but a recognition. Not of his title.

Of him.

She scribbled something as Ariela launched into another mythic tangent, and with a soft push of her gloved finger, sent the words drifting breathlessly across the courtyard.

Aurelian shifted slightly. Nothing visible. But the sound of wind caught the corner of his robe—

And the faintest flicker of a smile touched his cheek.

Chapter I — Academic Sparks

Year 2000, First Snow, 13th day — Embers swirling to a pulse.

The Old Sigil Hall smelled faintly of stone dust and scorched parchment—scent woven into the walls by centuries of spellcasting and mild academic mishaps. The ceiling vaulted high above, its support beams etched with historical glyphs that flickered during storms. Long tables filled the room in neat rows, each burnt with scratches and annotations from generations of overly curious students.

Helena sat with her satchel tucked beneath her bench, quill poised and eyes narrowed. The morning light filtered through stained glass windows in dusty reds and greens, casting soft glyph-like shapes across the floor. She hadn't been thrilled by the desk assignment: Lyla, a girl who challenged her at every turn, sat beside her. They had spoken in passing, worked together once during an enchanted language lab, and spent the rest of their shared time carefully not acknowledging one another.

Lyla sat with her arms folded, half-listening to the lecture while already sketching her own interpretation of the assignment glyph on parchment. Her movements were precise, deliberate. Her ink dried in sharp corners.

Professor Thassel droned from the front of the room, voice smooth and flat.

"Today's exercise: reconstruct a collapsed spell matrix. The glyph you see here—" he gestured, and a projection flared to life above his desk, "—has been derived from an original pattern lost to time. Your task is to determine its intent and complete it."

Whispers spread quickly. The shape on display was incomplete—a spiraling form, uneven and oddly bent at the edges. A fragment of something more complex.

Wynn, three rows back, leaned into Ariela and whispered something. The two giggled. Faye sat near the far column wall, seated alone by her own request. Her quill unmoving, her gaze drifting between the glyph and her classmates with the slow care of someone cataloguing each moment.

Helena studied the projection. Something was off. Lyla had already scribbled a potential resolution, angled perfectly to catch the professor's eye.

"You're going to overwrite the loop flow," Helena said without looking at her. "That stroke there? It forces closure."

Lyla didn't look up. "It balances the recursive strand."

"It erases it."

Wynn turned from her seat. "Are we arguing already? It's not even second bell."

Ariela grinned. "Feels like home."

Helena and Lyla kept working in parallel, neither conceding. But when Lyla finished her version and pushed her parchment forward to the projection circle, the glyph shimmered—then buckled inward, a faint snap of magical tension and the telltale puff of blue smoke.

Thassel didn't even look up. "Insufficient binding. Reset."

Lyla pressed her lips together.

Across the room, Wynn and Ariela were openly improvising.

"Dolphin again?" Ariela whispered.

"It's lucky," Wynn said, unfazed. "This time we're calling the flow the dorsal line. See? Cuts across the recursive field."

Ariela traced a swirl with a finger. "There. That's the tail—enchantment curve."

They activated their glyph. It shimmered, spun once—and settled into a surprisingly stable rotation. The room took notice.

Professor Thassel's eyes lifted. "A questionable metaphor. But effective. Pass."

Wynn grinned. "Told you."

Faye, meanwhile, had drawn an elegant, near-silent glyph using mirror-symmetry and layered curves. She did not raise her hand. She simply held it in view—perfect, motionless, glowing in a soft violet sheen.

Thassel nodded. "Stable. A textbook solution."

She said nothing.

Back at the front, Helena leaned forward slightly, squinting at the original spiral. Something about the twist at the centre—a loop that didn't terminate, but folded inward like a tightening ribbon—stirred recognition.

She pulled out her notebook.

A few pages in, she found it: a draft of a recursive loop she'd mapped during one of her sleepless nights. It wasn't identical, but the structure... it mirrored the anomaly in the projection. There was something *wrong* in the shape— wrong in a way that intrigued her.

She copied the diagram slowly. Modified one line. Adjusted the pressure on her quill. She felt the magic shift beneath her hand.

Her glyph didn't stabilize; it *breathed*.

The soulless shape pulsed once, then again. It didn't resolve —but it didn't collapse either. It looped; whispering something just on the edge of being language.

Faye, across the aisle, lifted her head slightly. Her eyes met Helena's—not in greeting, but in quiet approval.

Ariela's voice broke the quiet. "Professor? Was this from a real spell?"

Thassel's reply came slowly. "Not one we teach."

The bell rang.

Students stood, chairs scraping stone. They bustled out, grasping at flying papers and slinging half-packed bags over their shoulders. Wynn offered Helena a wink as she left, whilst Ariela trailed behind with a whistle on her lips. Lyla tidied up in silence, but not without a final unmasked glance toward her classmate's still-glowing parchment.

Helena lingered.

She turned back to the dimming projection, grasping a sharp etching wand firmly in her hand. She redrew the glyph again—smaller this time. Cleaner.

And when she returned to her desk…

There it was.

A small note on ripped paper, left where her inkpot had been. Neat script. No signature.

> *It folds back on itself. Look closer.*

She froze. Her heart didn't leap. It simply stilled with the quiet confidence of being noticed.

She folded the paper once, slowly, and slipped it into her sleeve.

Behind her, the last of the light from the spell glyph shimmered against the wall.

Chapter II — The Heartbeat

Year 2000, Deep Winter, 7th day

The spell wasn't alive, but it moved like something living

The following week, the class had been issued new assignments.

The forgotten glyph was not meant to be solved; it had too many permutations, and was possibly incomplete when the record was created. An ancient sketch, an experiment that led nowhere.

Professor Thassel had insisted as much when he set the assignment—a fragment of spell theory long thought to be unsolvable. But then again, he'd said the same thing about recursive binding matrices, and Helena had written a working draft of those last month.

So when the glyph shimmered into the air, spinning faintly above the professor's desk, Helena didn't see impossibility.

She saw invitation.

They worked in the west observatory. Aurelian had suggested it—quietly, without ceremony. Not as a prefect, but as a peer. Maybe he had other intentions. It was clear that this group was over represented by the more gifted members of the school.

> *"We need room,"* he said. *"And quiet, with no interruptions."*

Their friends came too. Wynn brought fig pastries. Ariela dragged in two extra chairs. Faye and Lyla offered commentary from the corner, half-invested, half-anxious.

Helena and Aurelian worked side by side, sketching iterations into the air with trailing glyph-light, arguing in murmurs, erasing, redrawing, shifting.

> *"This section doesn't decay,"* Helena said. *"See here—it pulses."*
>
> *"A delay glyph nested in a continuity loop,"* Aurelian murmured. *"But not for anchoring. It's behaving like..."*
>
> *"A heart,"* she finished.

He looked directly at her, his eyes brightly remembering late night notebooks shared with Helena.

The spell wasn't alive. But it *moved like something living.*

When they finished the construction, the glyph hovered just above the dais. Three spirals interlocking. A central sigil glowed red at its core—a shimmer that formed recursively; a detail that neither Helena or Aurelian had added intentionally.

The sigil pulsed once, causing a shimmer to radiate throughout the glyph.

Then again.

> *"It's not static," Faye observed, motioning closer.*
>
> *"It's not just pulsing," Lyla added, furrowing her brow. "It's choosing when."*

Ariela reached out toward the edge, and the light folded around her fingers like a rip tide.

> *"It feels... warm, heavy" bracing her arm against the tug.*
>
> *"It's stable," Helena confirmed. Her voice didn't shake, but her hands had stopped moving, her free hand lifting in a defensive posture.*
>
> *"Let it run," Aurelian commanded softly.*

The spiral responded.

`And time —          slipped.`

At first it was imperceptible. The room dimmed. The air stilled. Ariela's laugh echoed—but only for a moment too long. Wynn's gesture repeated. Lyla's breath looped in her throat.

The glyph pulsed. Then again. And again.

And again.

Reality began to echo.

> *"Something's wrong," Faye said. "The loop's binding us."*
>
> *"We're inside it," Lyla breathed. "It's using us to stay open."*
>
> *"I can't move my arm," Wynn said. "I mean, I can, but it resets."*
>
> *"Aurelian?" Helena asked.*

He was ahead already. Eyes focused. Hands flexing.

> *"I know. I'm ready."*
>
> *"You have authority," she said.*
>
> *"I won't do this without you. Without your permission." His voice hardened—pain swallowed just beneath the surface.*
>
> *"Then do it." Her eyes didn't waver.*

Aurelian lifted his hand. Not to cast, but to remember.

He traced a circle of glyphs in the air: + ¬ ! ? - 3 2 -

High up around the room, an alphabet of symbols carved deeply into the stones flared with light.

The Silence dropped like glass.

Each of their friends paused. Blinked. The spell collapsed inward, light folding like wings. The pulsing stopped.

Time— resumed.

Wynn, on her knees, rubbed her forehead.

> *"I feel like I dreamt something with teeth."*
>
> *"What just happened?" Ariela asked. "Was that part of the exercise?"*

Faye furrowed her brow. She looked directly at Helena, then turned toward Aurelian. She said nothing.

Lyla sat in silence; her eyes wide and dim, staring uncertainly at the floor.

> *"You fainted," Aurelian said gently offering his hand. "The spell destabilized. We ended it."*
>
> *"Don't worry," Helena added. "We'll make notes for the professor. All of us will get credits for this."*

Wynn frowned. But nodded. The others followed.

The others left the observatory carrying mildly wounded egos, steps unsteady, words hollow with something half-lost.

Helena and Aurelian remained to tidy the space and finish their notetaking. Once the others were gone, they spoke more freely.

> *"You did it cleanly," Helena said.*
>
> *"They won't remember the echo. Just the confusion."*
>
> *"And us?"*

Aurelian looked at the glyph etched faintly in the floor. Still glowing. Still warm.

> *"We'll remember for them."*

Helena didn't speak. She crossed over the glyph to stand beside him. He held out his hand.

Together, they etched the final line into the base of the leg beneath the observatory bench, and sat for possibly the longest moment of wonder that anyone had ever had.

Chapter III — Return to Work

Year 2000, Kindled Dusk, 10th day

Notes rewritten, pulse measured, silence made useful.

Aurelian sat in the corner, working a delicate scribing wand back and forth against a drafter's desk. The wand was fashioned from magisteel, the edge twisted down to the finest point imaginable—if not finer. A magnifying lens hovered above the workspace, shifting automatically as his gaze wandered, allowing for precise alterations to the glyphs etched below his hands. They pulsed gently with each stroke—not alive, not yet.

The dimly lit room, darkened by design, echoed softly with the ambient hum of sustained magic. Tools lay neatly arranged. Every surface shimmered with traces of use. The observatory was no longer a classroom.

It was a laboratory.

Helena sat cross-legged on the floor, the pages of her notebook illuminated by a soft light glyph overhead. She jotted down the results of the last run—margin notes, correction symbols, heartbeat sync patterns—then closed the book with a satisfied snap.

With a gleeful bounce and a practiced twirl, she rose, placed the filled notebook on a shelf already packed with dozens of identical volumes, and picked up a fresh one from the stack by the towering bookcase. She tapped the cover with her fingertip, imprinting today's date in soft gold.

Then she turned, bright-eyed, toward the centre of the circle —where Wynn stood barefoot on the etched sigil platform, her braid slightly frayed, her posture uncertain.

> *"Wynn, my dear, we're ready for you again."*

Wynn blinked. Her gaze drifted between Helena, the glowing spiral beneath her feet, and Aurelian's quiet form across the room. Then she looked at her hands.

> *"I... I thought we finished this already?"*

Helena gave a warm smile. Not unkind. But not quite comforting either.

> *"Almost. Just one more run. You were brilliant last time."*
>
> *"You said that last time."*

Aurelian looked up, just for a moment, and adjusted a tuning glyph on the wall. Wynn flinched slightly, though she didn't know why.

Helena stepped forward and gently offered her a warm cloth, which Wynn accepted without looking.

> *"Do you remember anything new this time?"* Helena asked casually.

> *"I... I had a dream. I think. There was a stone bench in the garden, beneath a willow tree. You were there. You asked me about time. I could hear a song, I sang it for you."*

Helena nodded thoughtfully and began writing.

> *"That's lovely, Wynn. Thank you. Let's see if anything else comes up."*

She gave a nod to Aurelian.

The glyph beneath Wynn shimmered.

And reset.

The loop would run again.

Not for the first time.

Not for the last.

But each time, Wynn would get a little closer.

And Helena and Aurelian would record.

Because knowledge wasn't free.

Not anymore.

Chapter IV — A Test of Motion

Year 2001, First Melt, 1st day

Resistance in motion, memory as mischief, refusal made art.

Ariela had to be caught.

That's how Helena phrased it. Not coerced. Not ordered. Caught.

She didn't like standing still. Not even in glyphlight.

She paced the edge of the platform, arms folded tight over her chest. She had removed her boots, but left her satchel slung at her hip. The symbols beneath her feet glowed faintly blue, less aggressive than before—but no less binding.

> *"I'm not answering riddles today," she said.*
>
> *"It's not a riddle," Aurelian replied from his corner. "It's a calibration."*
>
> *"Same thing. I hate quizzes."*

Helena stepped forward, calm, careful.

> *"Just a few questions. Like always."*
>
> *"How do I know they're always?" Ariela fired back. "You could've asked me a hundred times already."*

There was a pause.

Aurelian said nothing.

Helena gave the smallest smile. One that didn't reach her eyes.

> *"Do you remember anything from the last test?"*
>
> *"No," Ariela said quickly. Too quickly.*

Then she sighed.

> *"Except... I wrote something. Last night. In the corner of my math book. A glyph. It wasn't mine."*

Helena leaned forward.

> *"Do you still have it?"*

Ariela grinned.

> *"Nope. I burned it. Just to spite the voice in my head."*

Helena frowned.

Ariela's gaze softened, just a little.

> *"I don't know what this is. But whatever it is... you're not doing it to me. Not really."*
>
> *"And if we are?" Helena asked.*

Ariela shrugged.

> *"Then I hope you're scared. The professors won't stand for this if I tell them. Whatever it is your doing."*

She stepped off the platform.

The glyph didn't fire.

Aurelian blinked. Helena stared.

> *"How—?"*
>
> *"I stepped sideways," Ariela said, with a wink. "Not forward."*

And with that, she was gone.

Journal Entry : Helena

E#104, GC∆7 — Author: HH

Ariela isn't breaking through the spell. She's breaking around it. Keeping her silent is the least of my worries. She leaves breadcrumbs in threads I haven't traced. Reminds me of the way magpies circle trees before choosing one.

Wynn remembers nothing—except how she feels about remembering. Her singing soothes us. Her songs haunt me.

Faye sketches dreams she doesn't have.

Lyla asks fewer questions. But her answers are more complete.

They're catching up to us. Even now.

We are getting faster, but so are they.

I asked Aurelian if we should stop.

He said nothing.

Instead, he asked me if I could *still feel the first pulse.*

I could.

And that frightened me more than forgetting ever would.

Journal Entry : Aurelian

2000-FMT-SA-5200-AS

Helena had to take a reprieve this run.

Something Wynn said struck a chord.

I went to remind her that we have all the time in the world. That we should talk it through, but my own sadness welled as I thought of the toll this must be taking.

I let her go, and then sat with her on the floor by our bed ten minutes later.

We schedule 100 runs, then one day returns. To eat. To breathe. We sleep as much as we need.

We laugh. We joke. We play games.

This whole thing is a game.

But not really.

Our muses think they're helping voluntarily. Surely by now they must realise the trap.

They must sense it by now; in their bones, in their bodies.

But sensing isn't the same as escaping.

Maybe we are the ones who are trapped?

Was this our choice?

Was this always our intention?

Helena still supports me. I support her.

But we're new at this.

This moment won't last—unless we make it so.

The fear of it all slipping away is too much.

We must continue to seize this chance, until the end.

We've left ourselves no other way.

Chapter V — The Stillness Between Lines

Year 2001, Bloom, 6th day

Words that hum beneath silence, a drawing that dreams.

Faye no longer trusted silence.

Not because it was empty—but because it was too full.

She stood now at the centre of the observatory floor, fingers still stained with charcoal, sleeves rolled to the elbow. Her notebook was tucked under one arm, even though neither Helena or Aurelian had asked her to bring it.

She brought it anyway.

The platform beneath her feet shimmered faintly—not blue like before, but the pale violet of memory threads. A recent adjustment. Helena had suggested it would be gentler. Less like an interrogation. More like an invitation.

Faye didn't buy that for a moment.

Aurelian stood by the eastern wall, arms crossed. Helena sat this time, just outside the circle, her expression soft but unreadable.

> *"We're calibrating response drift,"* Helena said gently.
> *"You don't need to say anything you don't want to."*

Faye raised an eyebrow.

"Since when has that ever been true?"

Helena didn't respond. Aurelian didn't move.

Faye stepped forward into the circle and placed her notebook down.

"I drew these last night," she said.

"Not in a dream. Not in a trance. I just… kept drawing."

She flipped the book open.

Inside: spirals. Not perfect, but practiced. Shapes and symbols intertwined with margin scribbles. In one corner: a set of cursives no one had taught her. Helena instantly recognised them as glyphs they had experimented with in past loops.

She leaned closer, her voice careful.

"That one there. Where did it come from?"

Faye shrugged.

"I watched the shadow of my candle. It flickered in a pattern.

That pattern landed on my wrist. I traced it."

"You remembered it."

"No. I found it. That's different."

Aurelian stepped forward, studying the page.

> *"You knew it before. You drew it in Run Twelve."*

Faye didn't flinch.

> *"Then you already knew what I'd do today.*
> *Why bother testing me again?"*
> *"Because this time," Helena said softly,*
> *"you brought it willingly."*

The three of them stood in silence.

The glyph on the floor dimmed, then brightened.

Faye looked between them, then down at her drawing. She tapped the spiral with one finger.

> *"You're building something. I don't know what. But I*
> *know it matters. And I know it's costing you."*
> *"It is," Helena whispered.*
> *"Then stop using us like tools. Let us—let me help."*

Aurelian glanced toward Helena. A look passed between them—brief and indecipherable.

> *"What if we asked you to stay?" Helena said.*
> *"Fully. Beyond the runs. A conscious muse."*

Faye blinked. Her eyes dotting around the sterile room. Her voice, when it came, was quiet.

> *"Ask me again when you know who you're building it for."*

She picked up her notebook.

And walked off the platform.

Chapter VI — Fault Lines

Year 2001, Skybreak, 10th day

Lyla arrived before she was summoned.

She stood in the centre of the room, already inside the spiral, arms crossed, one eyebrow raised. Her uniform was impeccable. Her eyes, sharper still.

> *"You should try resetting your pattern," she said to Aurelian without looking up. "You're four degrees off centre."*

Aurelian looked up slowly. Said nothing. Adjusted the tuning glyph.

Helena entered moments later, coat still dusted with frost from the morning air. She paused at the doorway, took in the scene, and exhaled.

> *"We hadn't called for you yet."*
>
> *"I know. But I figured the story only works if I walk in uninvited."*
>
> *"The story?"*

Lyla smirked.

> *"The one you're writing. With us as muses."*

Helena gave a faint smile.

"You're not wrong."

The spiral beneath Lyla's boots shimmered in steady gold.

"Let me guess," Lyla said.

"Same questions. Same loop. You observe. We forget."

"You've been leaving anchor glyphs," Aurelian said plainly.

"On paper. On mirrors. In books. We found seven."

"Nine," Lyla corrected.

"The others are just better hidden."

Helena stepped forward.

"You're trying to breach the loop."

"I already have. I just don't remember it when I'm done."

She tilted her head.

"But I leave clues. And I've stopped trusting my handwriting.
That's usually a sign."

The room was quiet for a moment.

Helena tapped the corner of an adjacent dais, activating a memory pulse. Symbols appeared in the air, shimmered once, and stilled. The room inhaled—waiting for a response.

"What do you want, Lyla?"

"A seat at the table."

"And if we say no?"

"Then I keep testing. Just like you."

Aurelian folded his arms.

"You're not afraid?"

"Of forgetting? I've lived that fear.

Now I'm more afraid of what I remember."

"And what do you remember?"

"That you're building something beautiful. And dangerous.

And that I loved you both, once."

Helena blinked.

"Present tense or past?"

"I guess we'll find out in the next loop."

She stepped off the platform.

Aurelian looked to Helena.

"We should offer her the diagram."

"No," Helena said softly.

"Not yet."

"Then what do we do?"

Helena watched the spiral fade beneath Lyla's departing steps.

> *"We write a new question."*
>
> *"Sure," he replied, dryly. "But do I still need to offset by four degrees?"*

Helena laughed—not mocking, but fond.

> *"Of course! That's the strongest anchor we've established. I wouldn't change it in a thousand runs."*

He nodded, adjusting the dial without looking.

> *"Six thousand, seven hundred and ninety-two," he muttered. "And counting."*

Chapter VII — Release

Year 2001, Sunfall, 3rd day

Partings wrapped in sugared memories.

The professors waved oddly to the couple as they strode out of the prefects' briefing—less like instructors giving direction and more like colleagues exchanging courtesies. An uneasy familiarity lingered; the youngsters no longer seemed so young. They wondered whether the academy been too harsh on them.

Clutching their books and cautious not to show affection publicly, Aurelian put a deliberate bounce in his step, outwardly signalling his joy. Helena smirked at the floor.

Trust had been blooming between them. Everyone could see it, but none could prove more than the obvious. It mattered not, Helena thought—everything was in its right place.

From across the courtyard, Ariela called out:

> *"Is it done? Can I finally see?" she piped.*
> *"Of course!" Helena smiled brightly. "Right this way."*

Ariela

They led her to the old moss wall just past the south tower, near where the cliffs fell away into the distant pinewood haze. Most never ventured this far—too quiet, too forgotten, too still.

But Ariela had always liked the silence here.

It was the kind of quiet that waited with you, not against you.

Aurelian tapped the base of the wall. A tone rang out—like a bell subdued by velvet. Helena placed her palm on a moss-covered stone and whispered something that wasn't a word.

The stone parted.

Behind it: a narrow corridor, laced with green light. Dust motes suspended in the air like fireflies caught mid-thought. Vines brushed against their shoulders as they stepped through. A door appeared where there should have been sky.

Inside: a room filled with the smell of pressed herbs and polished leather.

A window that looked out onto no particular place, but felt exactly right.

And resting on a table: a compass.

Its casing was silver-gilt and worn with thumbprints. Its needle spun not toward north, but toward something personal. Something true.

> *"It's attuned," Helena said softly.*
>
> *"To what?" Ariela asked.*
>
> *"Desire," Aurelian replied. "It will take you wherever your heart most wants to go."*

Ariela's gaze flickered. She fell quiet as her pulse quickened.

> *"Even if I don't know where that is?" she breathed.*
>
> *"Especially then," replied Helena.*

Ariela stepped forward. Her hand hovered. The air smelled of oranges, sea salt, and a page just turned.

She lifted the compass.

The needle snapped into place.

And for a moment—one brief, perfect moment—she could feel it:

The *smell of freedom.*

The *sound of possibility.*

The *taste of adventure on her tongue*, bright as cider and sharp as stormwind.

She laughed—loud and sudden—and flung her arms around Helena first, then Aurelian, without asking permission.

"Thank you," she said. "Truly."

"Just promise to come back," Helena whispered.

Ariela winked.

"Not a chance."

She stepped out through the greenlight door, into the waiting world.

She'd still walk the threads of the academy.

But not the web of their spiral.

Later

In time, the compass would guide Ariela to lost cities and starlit peaks.

To riverbanks older than memory.

To taverns where strangers told her stories about herself.

She would feel the joy she always chased.

But then—one morning, without warning—the compass turned.

The needle spun and stopped.

Not toward treasure.

Not toward freedom.

But toward the one place she thought she'd never need again.

Back to the centre.

Back to the ones who had made her whole, and let her go.

> *The taste of adventure never dulled.*
>
> *But the bitterness of love always lingered.*
>
> *And the deep harmony of her realisation would echo in every step until she returned.*

⁞ **Excerpt from Helena's Journal** ⁞

Entry 8205-FALL-CT-9731-HH

Ariela's compass will not fail.

It never has. It never will.

I made sure of that.

I tuned it myself in the observatory's final light.

Aurelian set the brass. I laced the binding thread with a single, silent glyph of return.

Neither command, nor a leash, instead... permission.

When she turns homeward, it will not be because she was called.

It will be because she chose to come back.

And when she does—I will be waiting.

I will say nothing of the years. I will not measure the distance. I will not question where she's been or what she's done.

I will only speak the words I prepared the day she left.

> *"We left the light on. It's never gone out."*

She will laugh again.

And I will cry, perhaps.

But only a little.

Because I am patient.

Infinitely so.

┊ **Faye** ┊

They found her in the sunlit hallway near the scriptory alcove, where old ink clung to the flagstones and forgotten syllables still hummed beneath layers of dust. She had not asked to be released. She hadn't said much at all.

But Helena knew she was ready.

Faye followed without question, though her eyes never stopped reading the corridor walls. Even now, she mapped and noticed everything.

They took her to the oldest wing of the academy.

To the artist's tower—the one with the high-arched windows, the scent of oak soot and powdered chalk forever lingering in the floorboards. A place no one used anymore, save for the occasional poet too lost to be recovered.

In the centre of the room: a single stool. A long bench. A drafting table of deep walnut. And beside it, wrapped in velvet grey:

A silver-stitched art portfolio, soft with felt at the edges—its clasp shaped into a folded wing.

Helena unwrapped it without flourish. Inside: paper thick with magical resonance. The kind that absorbed more than just ink.

> *"These will remember your dreams," Aurelian said quietly.*
>
> *"The ones you don't recall when you wake."*
>
> *"They'll appear here," Helena added, "one sheet at a time. No matter where you are; it will find you. And if you ever forget who you are..."*

Faye stepped forward, slowly.

> *"Then I'll draw it back," she whispered.*
>
> *"Line by line."*

She picked up a sheet from the folio. Ran her fingers across the unmarked surface. Already, ink began to swell—gentle, hesitant, like a breath being taken.

Faye didn't cry. She had done that already, in a loop they never spoke of.

> *"Thank you," she said.*
>
> *"Don't thank us," Helena replied.*
>
> *"You drew the way forward. We just followed."*

Faye looked out the tall window. Then back down to the paper, now marked with the shape of a bridge, a river, and three birds that might have been glyphs.

> *"I'll stay for a while," she said.*
>
> *"Just long enough to draw myself whole again."*

When she was ready, she took the folio and walked into the golden light spilling through the corridor.

Her footsteps softer than ever before.

In the central observatory, Helena turned one page in a ledger no one else would ever read.

Faye's name remained.

But her signature—once etched beside every page number, each equation, and every correction—was gone. Erased by agreement.

Faye would remember herself.

But the invention would not.

> *"We'll carry this," Aurelian said.*
>
> *"For as long as it takes."*

Helena nodded solemnly, closed her log book, and tucked it away.

Wynn

Wynn didn't need to be fetched. She arrived on her own, arms full of something absurd—an enormous basket of tea cakes.

> *"I figured," she grinned, "if we're going to say goodbye, we should be well-fed doing it."*

Helena smiled before Wynn even spoke.

Aurelian looked up from the observatory ledgers and chuckled—something soft and rare, like rain just beginning on glass. He caught a tea cake thrust through the air towards him, it slowed near to him in a gentle arc.

> *"You're early," Helena said.*
>
> *"I'm always early," Wynn replied, placing the basket on the dais. "Except when I'm not. But those don't count."*

She looked around the room—the softly humming walls, the spiral etched into the floor like a heartbeat paused. She stepped to the centre with a gentle sigh and turned once in place, letting her fingers graze the air.

> *"You've kept it clean," she said.*
>
> *"We tried."*
>
> *"You've kept me safe."*

"We hoped."

Helena stepped forward, something hidden in her hands. Not wrapped. Not concealed. Just simple, and waiting.

A small golden locket, shaped like a spiral shell, no larger than a thumbprint.

"You used to hum a tune," Helena said.

"Every time the loop ended. We recorded it."

She opened the locket with a flick of her thumb.

A tune filled the room—simple, lilting, a little off-key.

Wynn closed her eyes.

"I don't remember writing it."

"But you always sang it," Aurelian said. "Every time. Without fail."

Wynn opened her eyes and accepted the locket, clutching it to her chest.

"Then I must've meant it."

"You did," Helena whispered.

"Will I forget again?"

"Not this time," Aurelian said. "This gift is outside the spiral."

"So I'll remember you both?"

Helena and Aurelian exchanged a glance. It held years.

> *"You'll remember how we made you feel," replied Helena, for the both of them.*
>
> *"And how we made you laugh." Aurelian added.*
>
> *"That's enough," Wynn said, her smile glowing. "That's everything."*

She threw her arms out and hugged them together—a tight, bright, and unashamed hug. The kind that required no apology. Then she waved with both hands, nearly dropping a cake on the way out.

> *"Oh! And I left a letter under your tea tray. It's very silly. Don't open it until I'm gone. Or do. Who cares? You never listen."*
>
> *"Thank you, Wynn."*
>
> *"You're welcome. Always."*

She skipped down the corridor, laughter echoing.

The spiral didn't even flicker.

She was *already* free.

When she was gone, Aurelian opened the observatory wall. Behind a panel of spellglass: a loop count.

14,532.

Every one of them had Wynn's voice on record.

Every one of them carried her laughter like a watermark.

They had passed the threshold of myth—and kept on walking.

Helena reached out and tapped the final entry.

Locked. Erased.

A spinning dial illuminated, erasing words and shapes from the spellglass, the number rapidly counting down to 0. The final digit lingered for a moment, then the glass faded.

The loop no longer held her song. It no longer needed to.

She had already sustained them with her joy.

> *"And now we give it back,"* Helena whispered.
>
> *"There's no price we'd dare accept in return."*

Wynn's Letter

Tucked beneath the tea tray, located moments after her departure. Unfolded together, while the smell of hot cakes lingered in the air.

To the pair of you,

I did think about making this dramatic. Something folded seventeen times and sealed in lavender wax.

But I thought, no. If I've learned anything in this beautiful strange place, it's that some truths should be simple.

So here it is.

I'm proud of you.

Not because of your cleverness.

Not because you challenged the impossible.

But because when it came down to it—you remembered to be kind.

You always made me tea, even when you didn't have time.

You always waited for me to catch up, even when we were already there.

You listened. You laughed. You let me matter. I felt the joy in our faces.

I would live all the loops again, if it meant I could be here with you.

I don't know where life will take me next. I don't need to.

Because I carry you both with me now.

In music. In memory. In joy.

Keep walking your spiral.

I'll be humming just ahead.

With love,

Wynn

P.S. If you ever find the blue marble, it's yours. You know where to leave it, if someone else needs it more.

⋮ **Lyla** ⋮

"Lyla, where are you?.."

The question echoed, unanswered, through the corridor beside the observatory.

Aurelian didn't move, but tapped his foot a single time impatiently.

Helena sighed a little sigh.

They both knew she'd arrive.

Lyla always arrived—but only when she'd finished rewriting the script in her head.

She entered without a word, her coat half-buttoned, hair pinned high like a crown she hadn't earned but wore anyway. She paused just inside the doorway, letting the quiet take her in.

"So," she said. "This is how you end it?"

"No," Aurelian replied. "This is how you continue it."

A desk had been cleared in the observatory. Nothing on it but a simple velvet wrapping, deep green. Lyla didn't need to be invited. She approached, drew the cloth aside, and revealed the book.

It was bound in old, dark leather, etched with a spiral motif barely visible until light hit it just so.

Not glowing. Weighty. Not enchanted. Just... complex.

She looked at them, one brow raised.

> *"What is it?"*
>
> *"Your ledger,"* Helena said. *"All of it."*
>
> *"My loops?"*
>
> *"Yes, a record of the loops,"* Aurelian said. *"But also your lives."*

She stared at it, fingers hovering.

> *"My... lives..."* she stuttered, *"At what cost?"*
>
> *"No cost,"* Helena replied. *"Not anymore."*
>
> *"And the catch?"*

Helena smiled from the corner of her mouth, but it wasn't cruel. She'd anticipated the suspicion, and the twist.

> *"It's a book that only you can read."*
>
> *"A book only someone who's lived many lives could comprehend,"* Aurelian added.
>
> *"It will take the rest of your life to understand; perhaps longer,"* Helena finished. *"And even then, it might still have secrets."*

Lyla picked it up. Heavier than it looked. She turned a few pages—not fast, not slowly. Just enough to glimpse something familiar. Something written in a hand not her own. Something she'd forgotten... *before* she wrote it.

With a bounce, she clutched the book to her chest. Not dramatically. Just so.

> *"You're not afraid I'll tell someone?" she quizzed.*

Helena shook her head.

> *"Who would believe you?"*
>
> *"No one," Lyla admitted, faintly exasperated.*
>
> *"We trust you. We'll always be here for you— somewhere. Wherever you need us."*
>
> *Aurelian's voice faltered, just slightly.*

She nodded once. Then again. Her usual smirk softened—not gone, but gentled.

> *"This was always the real gift, wasn't it?"*
>
> *"The story?"*
>
> *"The thank you, the recognition," Helena said quietly.*
>
> *"And the truth."*

Lyla nodded, turned and left without fanfare, book in hand.

No glow, and no glyph. Only Lyla—and the story only she could read.

Epilogue — The Observers

Year 2001, Sunfall, 4th day — Two remember what no-one recalls.

Helena and Aurelian returned to the spiral. He crossed the room from her, leaning silently against the bookshelf where they had kept their earliest notes, including Lyla's sharpest commentary—harsh words cut sharply into the margins.

> *"She'll start her own research now," Helena said.*
>
> *"Her glyphs always did feel unfinished," replied Aurelian.*
>
> *"She could outpace us."*
>
> *"We're on different paths now."*
>
> *"—Maybe one day those paths will intertwine?"*
>
> *"Maybe—if we let them," said Helena thoughtfully.*
>
> *"The professors can never find what we've created. The world must never know."*

The spiral beneath them pulsed once.

> *"Time to go. I'm needed at the prefect briefing, want to join me?" said Aurelian, reaching out with his hand.*

Together, they crossed the threshold out of the observatory's upper chamber. The door closed behind them with a soft click. As the lock met the clasp, a line of microscopic glyphs activated—dancing in pale gold like nerves beneath glass.

A quiet hum moved through the walls.

The pulse spiralled outward—first through the floor, then branching delicately between the grooves of hidden circuits. Threads of light danced across filaments of crystal and ink, touching each relay in turn.

At last, it reached the centre; it circled beneath a single wooden pedestal, carved from the same ash wood as their earliest wands. Resting on top was a glass case, unadorned.

Inside:

Two crystal gems, clear as frozen time.

Each shaped like an almond, small and delicate.

From each gem, a thread of twisted golden metal unspooled —two necklaces, perfectly symmetrical, their chains intertwined in a concentric spiral.

A shimmer circled beneath the pedestal once more. Around the room, all was in order. The tools of experimentation— neatly packed into clean, modern boxes. Delicate wands, annotated staves, memory-bound sigils, each encased within enchanted glass.

No portraits. No photos. No parchments taped across the walls.

No clippings from the past.

Just books, precisely bound and stacked in lines.

Then: crystal slabs, humming faintly.

And at the centre of everything—

A pulse,

A pedestal,

A spiral.

And the case that held their greatest invention; still to be unlocked.

Part III — The Sacred Invention

Chapter I — The Final Ordinary Thing

Year 2001, Lantern Light, 14th day

The evening sky bruised lavender. The outer stairwell of the observatory curled along the cliffside like a question mark left unspoken. The couple sat on the sun-warmed stone, just outside the highest alcove of the observatory, where the sky met the ridge in a band of faded gold.

The basket sat between them, still warm. Aurelian had insisted on real cloth napkins. Helena appeared to have brought too many cakes.

She picked one now—almond glaze, browned just a little too much—and bit into it without ceremony.

> *"You know," she said, wiping her mouth with the back of her sleeve, "this may be the last time we can pretend we're students."*

Aurelian raised an eyebrow.

> *"We have class tomorrow."*
> *"Yes, but not like this."*

He didn't disagree. He simply reached into the basket and produced his own: a flaky tart with sugared plums and a small, folded note from the bakery that read *have courage*. The kitchen staff often slipped notes like these in to deliveries—handwritten encouragements, a warm reminder that the academy always thought to care for its students.

He crumpled it, tucked it into his pocket.

Helena watched the horizon. The valley town below had begun to stir with lanterns. Somewhere in the courtyard, a lute plucked a half-familiar tune. Someone was late to supper. Another was laughing too loudly. The academy, in all its impossibly slow decay, was still alive.

> *"Do you remember the first time we drew a glyph together?" she asked.*
> *"The spiral."*
> *"It was never supposed to be symmetrical."*
> *"But it insisted."*

She smiled. It felt rare, but real.

> *"Everything changed after that," she said.*
> *"And everything stayed the same," he replied.*

A silence settled. Not comfortable. Not tense. Something else.

The space between endings and beginnings.

"You know," he said, softer now, "before I met you... the world seemed so ordinary. Not boring exactly. Just—linear. Predictable. But when you arrived, barrelling in here with your big ideas, challenging everything I thought I knew—that's when it all changed for me. When I think I fell in love."

Helena shifted slightly, gripping his hand, pressing her shoulder against his.

"Are you ready?" she asked.

"We've been ready for months!" he retorted brightly.

"That's not the same thing," she bristled, suppressing a smile.

Aurelian didn't answer immediately. He looked at the stars beginning to appear above the ridgeline. Cold. Precise. Familiar.

"I've prepared every variable," he said. "But I'm still afraid."

"Good," she whispered. "Then we won't be reckless."

She listened to the silence as her heart pulsed steadily, then continued:

"We don't get to unmake this."

"We won't need to," Aurelian replied without missing a beat.

"Even if it changes everything?"

"Especially then."

The light faded. The last warmth of the day drifted away. And still, they stayed. Until the cakes were gone, and the cold found their fingers, and the stars had fully revealed themselves.

Then, together, without ceremony, they rose.

They walked the winding staircase to the observatory door.

And as Helena reached for the lock, she said, so quietly even she could barely hear it:

> *"One last ordinary thing," she breathed—not sure if she meant the words, or if she wished they were true.*

Chapter II — The Binding

Year 2001, Lantern Light, 14th day

The spiral was never supposed to be symmetrical.

It was late evening. At the centre of the observatory, a crystal case gleamed—polished to a mirror shine—scattering light across the walls. The room felt different.

Not physically. The books still sat on their shelves, the chiselled floor still traced with careful runes— and the spiral at the centre of the observatory still gleamed softly beneath crystal starlight. But something in the air had shifted.

It felt like a held breath—ready for the last exhale before consequence.

Helena adjusted the sleeves of her coat. Aurelian was already working—his gestures precise, reverent. No dramatic flourishes. Just careful intention.

They stood on either side of the dais now. No longer students. No longer unknowing.

Just two minds. Two lives. Ready to *bind.*

> *"I guess this is it?" Helena asked sheepishly.*

Aurelian looked at her. Not like he was searching. Like he had *found* something, and was still learning how to carry it.

Her face was still young, but not untouched—marked by long nights, unspoken questions, the gravity of someone who knew how much things *could* matter. There was softness there; the kind that survived storms. The kind you trusted.

He shifted, rising briefly onto his toes. The kind of movement you make when stillness is no longer enough.

"I know it is. Because you're here with me."

Helena smiled closer, leaning ever brighter towards Aurelian.

He no longer needed hesitation. He adjusted the resonance ring on the pedestal. The spiral beneath them pulsed once— gold and soft. They both held their wands outstretched in symmetry, pointing along the spiralling glyphs on the floor. Eyes locked.

Then they both moved, almost perfectly in tandem.

As they drew the first stroke in the air—a line of sigils, each one balanced, each one resonating just faintly off-key. Sigils of rhythm, of memory, of intent.

They folded around each other. *Spoke* to each other.

"Now," Helena said. "Blood."

Aurelian withdrew the thin stiletto-shaped stylus. Touched it gently to his palm. The blood welled up the needle—not much. Just enough.

Helena mirrored him.

As the sigils activated a gust around them, Aurelian and Helena delicately mixed their blood together in the centre of the dais, the sticky red pool coalesced before spiralling along thin channels out towards the crystals.

As their blood met the surface of the twin crystals, a discordant pulse, like a bell made of light, rang through the room. *Blood magic was as sacred in the old way—quiet, final, not for show.* A deep bonding connection of the user to the spell at hand.

The clear gems flushed red—deep and radiant, like rubies just beginning to breathe. Glyphs burned across their surface, then vanished—*engraved inward.*

The circuitry, once etched across every wall of the observatory, began to ripple. Fold. Shrink.

Thread by thread, lines *flowed*—drawn inward toward the pulsing cores.

"It's working," Helena breathed.

Aurelian gently held the edge of the pedestal. His fingers feeling the pulse of the magic flowing past him.

"It's beautiful," he replied.

The crystals hummed. Then *spoke*—not with sound, but with resonance. Each pulse echoed with memory, pattern, recognition. A heartbeat. Two heartbeats. They could both hear them in sync with their own.

They'd built a living spiral. Intertwined.

The gems lifted from the dais, trailing golden chains as they rose. The necklaces flared open in perfect ceremony and settled across their shoulders. As the gems touched their skin, a bold thread of gold streaked out from the centre of their chests—light arcing across a darkened room, piercing the space between them. The thread tugged them together, almost pulling Helena off her feet, before fading. Aurelian steadied himself on the dais and reached across to give Helena a gentle kiss. She closed her eyes. The kiss stayed, even after it ended.

They stepped back.

"Ready, my love?"

"Always."

They tapped the gems... and time stopped.

Chapter III — The Spiral Wound

Year 2001, Shadows, 19th day – Five seconds lasted three days.

Night curled around the academy's courtyard, casting long shadows from flaming torches. They were about to create a moment that would last longer than it had any right to.

The first remote activation was unceremonious.

No dramatic flares. No public announcement. Just two former students standing on old stone beside a frost-laced sundial, faces warmed by the bakery's latest batch, scarves looped twice for comfort. The courtyard was empty. The moment chosen. The necklace chains already warm against their skin. It had taken great effort to arrange a meeting— quiet messages passed between crowded class schedules.

Helena's fingers found the gem at her throat.

Aurelian mirrored her, watching her movements closely.

They exchanged no words. Only a glance.

A silent agreement between those who had already passed through too many thresholds.

Together, they pressed the crystals.

And the world *stopped*.

It didn't shatter. It *paused*. A glisten of octarine pooled near the edges.

The wind, already gentle, froze mid-gust. Motionless like a perfect photograph.

A bird in the distance hovered in stillness, wings fully open, never flapping.

Even the fountain behind the west tower—forever sputtering, leaking, mumbling its glyphs—had stilled to a delicate column, caught like glass blown in mid-form.

The spiral *held*.

They stood in the centre of it.

No noise. No motion. Only the thrum of their own heartbeats reaching their ears.

Only each other.

And the reassuring, slow pulse of the red gems at their chests, matching their own.

> *"We're in," Aurelian said, voice too loud in the stillness.*

Helena didn't speak. She reached out, and touched the water mid-air. It did not ripple. It was *hard.* Cold. Absolutely unmoving.

> *"The portable Spiral is stable," she whispered.*

> *"How long do we stay?"*
>
> *"Until we're done,"* she said.
>
> *"What does done mean?"*

She turned to him with that half-smile—the kind only someone who has outlived a dozen lifetimes can wear.

> *"We'll know when the world is ready for us again."*

They tested everything they could think of.

Glyphs drawn mid-air hung in place, light frozen in curving loops.

Pages of notebooks could be read, but not turned.

Tea brewed, but never steeped.

They could walk. Speak. Think. Touch.

But nothing else could.

> *"It doesn't affect memory,"* Helena noted. *"Not ours. Not yet."*
>
> *"Then we begin mapping the edge."*

They measured where the spiral ended. They removed the necklaces and hung them on the branch of a tree. Thirty feet. Then thirty-five. Then a soft shimmer—a sound like breath through silk—and they found the limit.

Just past the south archway, a leaf suspended in air dropped the moment Aurelian passed beyond the radius. Time resumed in slices, thin as vellum.

> *"It's not a prison,"* he observed.
>
> *"No,"* Helena agreed. *"It's a room."*
>
> *"A place we can take with us."*

They stayed for three days.

Inside five seconds.

They read six books. Rewrote their anchoring glyphs. Added two entirely new failsafes. Slept twice. Ate all the cake.

The gems dimmed slightly on the third day. That was the warning. A gentle red pulse that faltered, *just once.*

Helena touched her crystal. Aurelian did the same.

Together, they stood still—anchored—while time rushed back around them like wind swirling through a mountainous valley.

A bell rang far across the courtyard.

A student sneezed in the library window.

A page turned. A lantern flickered.

Glyphs they'd written fizzled into the moving air.

And no one knew what had just been done.

"We need to pretend we've been here the whole time," Helena said, casually brushing cake crumbs from her scarf.

"We were," Aurelian replied. *"In a manner of speaking."*

"No more than a moment should pass next time," she added. *"For the sake of appearances."*

"We could do a month. We'd need to find a stronger source of magic."

"But should we?"

He didn't answer.

He just looked toward the stars.

Then back to her.

Then at the next variable—quiet, pulsing, inevitable.

Chapter IV — Rules of the Device

Year 2002, Deep Winter, 10th day – Investigatory log.

Confirmed behaviours, recorded for consideration.

⋮ Synchronisation Lock ⋮

Observation

Activation of either crystal initiates the Spiral for both bearers, regardless of distance.

Demonstration

Helena activated hers during solitary study. Aurelian was three buildings away, sketching field notes.

She walked through frozen air until she reached him in the west garden. His field merged seamlessly with hers on visual contact. No resistance. No disruption.

> *"You started early," he said.*
>
> *"I wanted silence first," she replied.*
>
> *"Then I'll enter gently."*

Conclusion

Each bearer maintains their own individual field. Overlap merges the fields into the Spiral. Distance is irrelevant. No decay detected on merge.

Return Point Fidelity

Observation

On exit from the Spiral, each bearer returns to the precise location and moment of their individual activation.

Demonstration

Helena paused mid-step on the bridge. Aurelian stood in the observatory atrium. They entered, spent eight subjective hours reviewing vault annotations.

When they released, Helena resumed her stride. Aurelian blinked, arm still folded. To all others, nothing had changed.

Conclusion

Return locks the bearer's physical position to their point of activation, but all intervening environmental and personal changes persist. Only *location and chronology* reset — not consequence.

Temporal Parity

Observation

Time progresses equally for both bearers during the Spiral, regardless of awareness or activity. Dilated time remains synchronised like heartbeats in tempo. Synchronisation ensures parity. Users must respect the shared field unselfishly.

Demonstration

Aurelian slept. Helena worked. He awoke hungry and weary. Her ink was dry, her notes complete.

> *"You moved the sun while I dreamed,"* he said.
> *"We both paid the hours,"* she replied.

It mattered little that they had shared each other's presence only in sleep.

Conclusion

Activation does not pause internal time. Biological, cognitive, and magical processes continue normally. Subjective time is lived equally.

Independent Invocation, Mutual Effect

Observation

Either bearer may initiate the Spiral unilaterally. The effect is applied to both without prompt or refusal.

Demonstration

Aurelian activated his crystal during a walking meditation. Helena, mid-lecture, entered immediately.

Her chalk paused in midair. A student's laugh froze mid-breath.

> *"I was mid-sentence." she said.*
> *"You always are." he replied.*

Conclusion

No signalling required. No gesture needed. The link is always listening. The bond itself is sufficient.

⋮ **Exit Dependency** ⋮

Observation

Both bearers must release the Spiral for time to resume.

Demonstration

Helena lingered. Aurelian prepared for exit. The field held. His crystal dimmed but did not release.

He returned to her. Waited. When she was ready, Helena released her lock.

Conclusion

Exit is cooperative. Unilateral release is not permitted. Spiral maintains lock until both bindings are voluntarily surrendered.

Emotional Neutrality

Observation

Spiral activation is unaffected by mood, emotional drift, or personal conflict.

Demonstration

They had argued earlier that day—brief, but sharp. Helena activated without preamble. Spiral accepted both.

They did not speak for several hours, but completed all assigned research with perfect coordination.

> *"We are still excellent," he said.*
> *"We are still aligned," she replied.*

Conclusion

Emotion is not a factor in activation. The Spiral reads structure, not sentiment. The link persists regardless of feeling. While emotional state does not influence Spiral activation, prolonged occupancy may lead to emotional attenuation, memory flattening, or affective lag — side effects of extended time asymmetry.

Field Merging

Observation

Although activation is shared, initial positions may differ. Bearers may enter the Spiral from separate locations and rejoin at will within the frozen world.

Demonstration

Helena activated her crystal while in the observatory. Aurelian, already in the west gardens, was brought into the Spiral immediately.

They began the loop apart, walking separately through paused corridors and breathless spaces. Twenty-three minutes later, they met at the sundial.

Neither had aged unevenly. Their gems pulsed in rhythm.

> *"It's still strange," she said.*
> *"The world has no memory of our paths," he replied.*
> *"Only us."*

Conclusion

All Spiral activity occurs within a unified temporal field. Entry points may be distinct, but movement is unrestricted. There is only one root Spiral per invocation.

| Persistence & Acceleration |

Observation

All changes made within the Spiral persist in the outside world. Physical, magical, and environmental manipulations are real — only their passage through time is veiled.

Demonstration

Aurelian bent steel and carved runes into stone. Helena planted a birch grove from seed. They returned, palms raw, chests heaving — and the world resumed with the changes in place. The stone was shaped. The trees remained.

> *"You built a house," she said.*
> *"I had the time," he replied.*

Conclusion

The Spiral does not pause the world; it displaces the bearers into accelerated temporal density. The illusion of stillness is the world's lag, not ours. All Spiral work is real work. All time within must be earned, paid, and remembered.

Temporal Sizing

Observation

Initial Spiral activation encompasses *only* the bearer. The field expands from a singular locus and does not automatically include others — even those in immediate proximity. Expansion is possible but must be executed deliberately and within established thresholds.

Demonstration

Helena initiated the Spiral in the lecture hall. All others remained outside the field, frozen mid-breath. She walked among them undetected, her gem pulsing at baseline intensity. With concentration, she expanded the radius to envelop a single student — slowly, carefully.

The moment the field reached the student's edge, the Spiral hesitated. The student twitched — not fully frozen, not fully aware. The field reasserted itself. The student stilled.

> *"Too fast,"* Helena murmured.
> *"Too close,"* Aurelian added later.

Conclusion

Careless enlargement of a personal field may result in partial inclusion — a dangerous liminal state for the uninitiated that may lead to unintended trauma.

Activation Limit

Observation

Activation and maintenance demand a steady, ambient source of magic. The field does not self-sustain—it draws upon a foundational energetic substrate present beneath all living matter and thermal flux. Environments high in heat, motion, or biological activity are ideal. Sterile or inert spaces (e.g. vacuums, necrotic zones) weaken or prevent formation.

Demonstration

Helena attempted ignition in a basalt crypt long emptied of life. The crystal flickered and failed. Repeated efforts drained the chamber's warmth—her breath fogged, her fingertips numbed, scarf frosting over. Only after significant thermal loss and cellular fatigue did the field stabilize.

By contrast, adjacent to a live elemental core, Aurelian activated the field nearly instant. It endured without drain for five subjective days; no visible biological degradation occurred.

> *"We burned a year's worth of summer in a single breath,"* Helena noted.
>
> *"Then let's plant something when we're done,"* Aurelian replied.

Conclusion

Magic is fuel; the field is fire. Without adequate energy, it collapses or strips power from its surroundings. Operation drains local energy—thermal, biological, emotional. Prolonged use in barren or lifeless zones causes entropy: withering plants, chill air, exhaustion in nearby creatures.

Mitigation

With an internalised energy source—a magically stabilised miniature stellar core—the strain can be offloaded. Such an anchor supplies radiance, motion, magical heft even in inhospitable places.

> *"We carry our sun in our pockets now," Helena wrote.*
>
> *"It hums when I'm afraid," Aurelian added.*

⁞ **Advisory** ⁞

Device activation without energy buffering in low-magic environments is hazardous. Bearers may experience accelerated fatigue, cognitive fog, temporal drift or life-force depletion. This is not theoretical. Losses have occurred.

Observation

In a muddy hillside grave, frozen ground despite daylight, Helena gripped her arm—perhaps letting life's warmth slip. The device had consumed lifeforce nearby before lashing out: almost petrifying her arm. A stray goat, used as test, suffered fully.

Conclusion

Utmost care is required around organic life. A gradual shutdown protocol is in place: dilated fields must be collapsed smoothly rather than allowed to become an all-consuming vortex. Damage to living beings must be minimised.

Addendum: Temporal Wear

Observation

Extended occupancy within the Spiral produces significant biological strain. While tissues remain intact, subjects report progressive fatigue, memory bleed, and chronometric dissonance. The body ages in real time. The world does not.

Demonstration

After an extended navigation of Spiral protocols lasting eleven subjective weeks, Helena collapsed from synaptic overload. Aurelian, though stable, emerged visibly aged. He initiated external stasis to preserve continuity.

> *"We are brilliant," she said, wrapped in bandage and silence.*
>
> *"Stop bleeding brilliance for a moment," he replied, his voice cracking.*

Conclusion

A corrective was developed: a regeneration binding worn on the skin. *The Band,* when properly tuned, arrests cellular degradation, heals acute trauma, and sustains bearer integrity under extreme time dilation. The band offers no immortality—only maintenance. Removing the band appears to have no immediate ill effect.

Addendum: Silencing

Observation

Spellwork cast at or near the Spiral's boundary remains in temporal stasis until the field collapses. Upon release, such spells activate instantly, preserving intent and trajectory. Alternatively, spells may be fully executed *within* the Spiral, assuming sufficient field volume and duration. Both approaches risk detection if observed by the uninitiated.

Demonstration

Aurelian placed a glyph at the threshold—half in, half out. Upon collapse, the spell resolved with no delay, striking its intended mark. The effect was clean, but *too visible.*

Helena, working within a fully expanded field, completed a memory obfuscation ritual on a groundskeeper who had entered the radius before compression. The man's awareness was severed mid-thought. Upon field collapse, he blinked, turned, and resumed sweeping.

> *"He saw us," Aurelian said.*
> *"Not anymore," Helena murmured.*

Conclusion

Temporal manipulation is not invisible to all. Chance encounters, incidental witnesses, or delayed spell effects may lead to Spiral exposure. In such cases, *silencing* is mandatory. Methods vary — memory erasure, mental warding, localized amnesia sigils — but the outcome must be consistent: *no knowledge must remain.*

Bearers are advised to maintain tight field control in populated areas. While the Spiral bends time, it does not erase consequence. The cost of discretion is often paid in silence.

Failure to act in time may result in memory paradox, psychic trauma, or undesired propagation of forbidden knowledge. In all cases, *containment is paramount.* Note: if unsure, simply reactivate the field, and reapply silence.

Chapter V — Echoes of Power

Year 2002, Twilight Harvest, 12th day

The Spiral leaves no record... except in kindness.

They returned to the rhythm,

still, the bells rang,

still, the sky opened,

still, the world required lunch and laughter and light.

Magic or not, the leaves kept falling.

⋮ **Twilight Harvest, 12th day** ⋮

Greenhouse corridor. Morning mist. A dropped jar of seedlings.

It slipped from a first-year's hands as they passed the heavy door. She hadn't meant to startle the assistant walking past, but their shoulders clipped and the jar—unglazed clay, still warm from the kiln—tumbled out of her bag.

It did not break—it never touched the ground.

She didn't notice.

The assistant gave her a sharp look, and she offered a clumsy apology, clutching the jar tighter.

Helena watched from the far side of the greenhouse, through panes clouded with condensation and thyme steam.

She did not smile. She simply whispered:

> *"That's one more."*

Aurelian, unseen behind a stack of seedling crates, nodded without speaking.

The air carried the faint scent of rosemary and lightning.

Filed.

No further action.

Lantern Light, 9th day

East Colonnade. Morning frost. A step too quick.

Tomas was late.

Not in a catastrophic way. Just enough to feel the day folding in wrong around the edges. His scarf wouldn't sit right. His boots were too stiff. The bread he grabbed from the commons had gone slightly stale.

He didn't think of much as he crossed the colonnade.

Just the usual thoughts:

> *Did I get the right star chart?*
>
> *Was today the fire-safety lecture or the familiar ethics seminar?*
>
> *Did anyone else smell burnt sage in the dorm last night?*

His bag was too full. Slung wrong.

His foot hit the second step too quickly.

There was frost.

He slipped.

But his bag didn't spill.

And he didn't fall.

His left foot found the next step like it was *waiting* for him. His body twisted, then straightened, as if nudged gently by a memory he hadn't had yet.

He blinked.

Clutched his satchel tighter.

Kept walking.

Helena leaned back from the corridor wall, exhaling quietly. She made no mark. No motion.

Aurelian, two floors up, noted the pulse from his gem but didn't comment.

Filed.

Tomas Halren. Morning route trace. Spiral activated for four seconds.

Intervention: micro-correction of balance and satchel angle.

Subject unaware. Residual confidence elevated. Spiral closed cleanly.

Frostfall, 3rd day

Library sublevel. Evening glow. Two students reading the same sentence at the same time.

They sat at opposite corners of the same long table. Neither noticed the other for nearly an hour.

But both had pulled the same volume. Both were tracing the same passage. Both tilted their heads at the same time.

Aurelian passed behind them, steps silent. He paused— noted the page: a treatise on mirrored perception in recursive charms.

One student yawned. The other stretched. Still, neither looked up.

Helena arrived later and ran her finger along the spine.

> *"Is it active?" she asked.*
>
> *"Not yet," Aurelian replied. "But something is resonating."*

They left it alone.

Let it hum.

Filed.

No contact made. Passive harmonic observed. Recommend periodic sweep. Low priority.

┊ **Shadows, 14th day** ┊

Laundry hall. Dusk. Warm stones underfoot, steam in the rafters.
A near-electrocution.

The hall buzzed with the low hum of enchantment—sigils stitched into the stone to heat water, spin clothes, dispel damp. Most of them were older than the students using them. Some had been updated. Some had not.

One student—Letha, second year, practical, precise—was trying to fix a jammed drying basin. A sock had gotten caught in the glyph track. Again.

She reached in too far.

Didn't notice the filament of static curling around the basin rim. A leftover charge. Harmless to the machines.

Less so to her.

Helena was nearby, half-listening to a conversation about boiling linen without discharging spirit-bonded inks.

The thrum from her crystal shifted—barely. Not an alarm. Just a hum, low and living.

She moved without hurry.

By the time Letha's hand passed the glyph boundary, the charge was gone.

112

Redirected. Dissolved.

The sock came loose.

Letha blinked, looked at her fingers, and frowned.

She never noticed the lack of shock—only the fact that the machine finally listened.

Aurelian, above, near the western eaves, felt the same pulse pass through his ribs.

> *"That one?" he asked.*

Helena didn't look up.

> *"No harm done."*

Filed.

Letha Corren. Minor field adjustment. Environmental correction within Spiral latency threshold. Subject unaware. No injury. No follow-up.

Shadows, 17th day Tea with Friends

The world resumes. The winds strengthen, and the days begin to shorten. No one forgets, not really, not entirely.

They met for tea again.

The table near the east window was available, as it always was on Thursdays. The mugs were chipped in familiar places. The sunlight filtered through the leaves in angles they all quietly acknowledged but did not name.

Ariela was telling a story that couldn't possibly be true.

Wynn was crying, but only from laughter.

Faye was sketching a moth on the corner of a napkin.

Lyla was rereading the menu like it might confess something new.

Helena arrived first.

Aurelian arrived last.

They didn't speak of the Spiral. Not directly. But there were gestures—careful pauses. A knowing glance as Wynn stirred her tea the wrong way three times. The way Ariela's compass always faced slightly to the left of true north, even indoors. The way Lyla's book pulsed, faintly, at the edge of audible thought.

These were no longer *loops.* They were *habits.*

Traces. Resonances.

They lived in the world again.

But the world had *adjusted.*

Their table was approached by a wandering professor, curious to see such luminous students gathered for polite conversation. They nodded in approval for such mature, refined behaviours. "Treasure these memories, the academy can only hold you for long."

They said thank you, a laugh broke out among them, like ice breaking. Helena and Aurelian looked to their tea cups, embarrassed at the absurdity. *They were* only just beginning their lives here. Their friends, the professors, would live much shorter lives by comparison.

At the end of tea Faye reached out to Aurelian, almost touching his hand, forgetting for a moment her place. Terrified she almost slapped it away before a blink. Helena activated the spiral, forced Aurelian to reassert himself, then brought Faye in to recompose herself, reminding her of her situation, and then asked her to proceed.

Time resumed.

Faye reached out to Aurelian, "A word if I may?", glancing to the floor. The others trailed off away from the dining hall. Stood by the tea table, overlooking the gardens.

> *"Anything, any time for you Faye".*
>
> *"Good catch, sorry to embarrass you".*
>
> *"They mustn't know. You have a normal life to lead. If you stray too close you will be burned."*

The statement seemed wholly poetic if not for the literal implications.

> *"I know. I know," she steadied, "I give everything to see my sister again, but also to be in your grace."*
>
> *Aurelian smiled kindly. "Not long now, autumn is almost over. Never let us keep you from loved ones."*
>
> *"Is it so wrong?", she stuttered. "To love."*
>
> *"Just know not to confuse loyalty for love, I can only hold you so close".*

Faye relented, supressing a tear, her calmness faltering. "If I had known, I would never have held back".

> *"We learn too late, but I promise, there will always be time".*

He held her hand briefly from a far—then let it drop. "Go on, you're needed" he said, as Wynn turned to call her.

Shadows, 18th day — A Letter from Faye

Sent via silver post, crisp envelope, addressed with practiced care.

Dear Elsie,

I hope this letter finds you well—and early, for once. I remember last year's winter post disaster and how the snow turned your ink into something resembling runes. You claimed it was a secret language only I could decode. I still have that letter.

The academy is... demanding. Not in the way the brochures promised, either. The kind of demanding that happens slowly—like being carved into someone more specific than you thought you were. But I'm doing well. I've made friends. Or rather, I've found people worth learning beside. That's enough, I think.

I won't bore you with talk of glyphs or spells (unless you ask, and then I'll send you diagrams you can proudly ignore). Instead, I'll say this:

I miss you.

Every day.

Not just for the jokes, or the way you make the world feel less heavy when I forget how to hold it—but because I still wake up sometimes expecting you to be in the next room, muttering about misbuttoned uniforms and sneaking toast into your coat pocket.

You're not here.

And I've grown older in a way I can't explain.

But I'll be home soon. A few more weeks. Maybe less. We'll have tea. We'll make too many biscuits. We'll walk until our legs ache and our mouths do too from all the talking.

I can't wait.

With all my love,

Faye

First Snow, 1st day — Elsie's Reply

Delivered three days later on pale crumpled paper.

Hi Faye!

I've read your letter three times already, and I keep making mum read the bit about me sneaking toast. She says I'm "exposed," but I say it's "archival truth."

I'm glad you're okay. And I know you can't say everything, but I know you. So I know there's more. And I'm not going to press. Because I trust you. And you'll tell me when you can.

Things are boring here. In the best way. Dad finally fixed the leak in the conservatory, so it's only slightly raining indoors now. Mum's making pear preserves again (she says it's for you, but we both know I've eaten half already).

You'll be home so soon. Just a few more weeks. That's barely anything. I'm counting down. I've made a paper chain and everything.

I miss you every day.

Come home safe.

Love,

Elsie

P.S. I'm still keeping your spot in the garden chair. No one else is allowed to sit there. Not even me.

The Moment

Faye sat on the edge of her narrow bed.

The dormitory was quiet—just the soft hush of a charmed candle and the gentle creak of old timbers. She unfolded the letter carefully. Smoothed it flat.

Her fingers trembled before her heart did, and then the first sob broke without warning.

An open cry that swept through her chest.

A release that came from someplace below memory.

She curled around the page, not to shield it from the world, but to stay close to it. Her forehead against the words. Her tears soaking into the sentences that didn't know how much time she had lost.

That paper chain? She would count every link.

Every night until she could cross the final threshold, unlooped, unseen.

Free.

And finally home.

First Snow, 19th day — Departure day

Clouds watching.

Two weeks later, brooding clouds gathered over the peaks—dark and deliberate, heavy with ice waiting to fall. The air smelled of old frost and new silence.

Faye had packed the night before. Now she waited.

Her coach—a private, crested thing drawn by enchanted horses—had been arranged by the academy. *"To protect our finest students." "To honour the distances many have travelled." "To ensure the greatest care in their return."*

Her mother had been elated.

The kind of relief that could breathe again.

No train stations. No jostling spells. Just silk curtains and safe passage.

She didn't need it, of course.

Faye was brilliant. Measured. Capable.

A mage of her calibre would walk untouched through any street, and the street would *know to behave.*

And yet.

To Faye, the gesture felt like a leash. Soft. Padded. But a leash all the same.

A direct line home.

A clear path, paved by other people's decisions.

And at the end of it: her sister. Her family. Her *longing.*

Perhaps she was overthinking.

Aurelian and Helena hadn't used the Spiral on her since that last tea. No pulsing gems. No unspoken loops.

Time had moved forward. *Naturally.*

But still—Faye could feel something Helena once said, echoing inside her:

> *"This moment is just a grain of sand, atop the mountain of your lifetime."*

It had been *so long.*

And in her heart, Faye wasn't just yearning.

She was *starving.*

The snow began to fall.

Chapter VI — Snowbound Homecoming

Year 2002, Last Ice, 20th day

Timeless snow, without the magic—and the shape of home.

Snow had begun to fall again.

Not the sharp flurries of early autumn, but the soft, deliberate kind that arrived with winter's first true breath. It blanketed the academy's rooftops in quiet grace, dampening sound, sharpening light, turning every path into something freshly drawn. Helena stood beneath the archway of the eastern gate, her travel cloak dusted white, a single finger tracing the edge of her packed satchel.

"They'll be watching from the window," she said.

Aurelian adjusted the collar of his coat, smiling. "Only every five minutes."

She exhaled into the cold, breath clouding between them.

> *"We can't Spiral this."*
> *"Wouldn't dream of it."*

They departed on foot, as promised, the path winding down from the academy ridge through forested silence. No magic was required. They walked onwards—silent beneath the hush of soft white snow.

The journey took them a day and a half, with overnight rest at a village inn where the innkeeper mistook them for newlyweds. Helena laughed. Aurelian blushed. They did not correct him.

When they reached her childhood home, it was late morning, and the snow had only thickened. Her parents were already on the porch.

Her mother, cheeks pink from cold, enveloped her in a hug that made Helena small again. Her father, silent at first, offered Aurelian a handshake that lingered just a moment too long before breaking into a smile.

> *"Welcome to the north," he said. "We hope you're hungry."*

They stayed four nights.

Helena took her old room, its walls still etched with constellation charts and half-finished sigil diagrams. Aurelian was given the guest room beside the hearth, where a sleepy old dog insisted on curling against his boots each evening.

Meals were warm, stories warmer. Her parents were gentle with their questions, sharper with their observations. They noticed how Aurelian never quite looked away from Helena when she spoke. They noticed how Helena sat straighter when he entered the room.

On the third night, Helena's father found Aurelian in the garden shed, quietly re-enchanting the rusted tools without being asked.

> *"You love her?" he asked, without preamble.*

Aurelian looked up, surprised but not unsettled.

> *"I do."*
>
> *"Then let it show when it matters. The world she carries is heavier than most."*
>
> *"I know. I carry it too."*

They shook hands again. This time, it was enough.

When they departed, her mother tucked wrapped gingerbread into Helena's satchel. Her father insisted on walking them to the trailhead, boots crunching in the frost.

> *"Next time," he said, "stay longer."*
>
> *"Next time," Helena replied, and meant it.*

Aurelian's parents lived in a coastal town where the snow melted into sea fog before it could settle. The house sat low and wide against the cliffs, windows open to salt air and the sound of waves.

His mother embraced Helena like a daughter the moment she stepped through the door. His father, tall and slow-spoken, welcomed them with spiced cider and a warmth that came from steady living.

Here, they were not asked to sleep apart.

Aurelian's room had changed little over the years—a constellation globe still sat spinning beside the bed, a bookshelf bowed under the weight of magical theory and old sea myths. Helena took the left side of the bed without a word.

They spent five days there.

Long walks by the cliffs. Lazy breakfasts. An afternoon spent helping Aurelian's father patch a leaky roof sigil. Evenings filled with tea and questions, stories and laughter. There was no need to Spiral. No need to hide.
On the final night, Aurelian's mother found Helena staring out at the sea.

> *"He was always waiting for someone to match him,"* she said, folding a shawl over Helena's shoulders.
>
> *"Was I the one?"*
>
> *"You were the one who didn't flinch."*

They watched the tide pull against the rocks, moonlight gilding each wave.

> *"Thank you,"* Helena whispered.
>
> *"Thank you,"* came the reply.

They left before dawn—exchanging quiet gratitude at the porch. The snow did not follow them this time. Only the wind. And the warmth in their chests that would not dim, not even in the Spiral.

Chapter VII — Entanglement

Year 2002, First Melt, 6th day

They moved like memory — too perfect to question.

The courtyard was busy for a weekday. Students scattered across stone benches and shaded steps, eating, sketching, gossiping. Pale spring light stretched long shadows across the ground. Somewhere, someone had managed to bring a kettle outside and was boiling water with a soft hum of spellheat.

Helena and Aurelian sat together on the bench nearest the sundial. Their books were closed. Their satchels untouched. Helena had a slip of paper folded between her fingers, which she kept turning over, again and again. Her eyes were scanning the courtyard.

"There," she said quietly.

Aurelian followed her gaze. Faye had just arrived. She was alone, arms full of scrolls and notebooks. She passed the stone archway and paused briefly, looking left, then right. Her brow furrowed slightly. Something about the way she moved said she was retracing steps.

"She's remembering the wrong day," Aurelian said.

Helena nodded. "That conversation we had beside the fountain? We didn't have it. Not in this strand."

He looked at her. "Did you speak too early?"

"I might have. She reacted as if she already knew."

A quiet chime sounded on Helena's ring. She held her hand out, pressing a small glyph carved into the silver. Around them, time… slowed. Not stopped. Just enough to create space. The courtyard blurred at the edges. Sound dulled.

Aurelian stood up from the bench.

Together, they crossed the courtyard. Faye remained still mid-step, frozen in a half-turn toward the north wing.

"I didn't think we'd need to adjust this one," Aurelian said, eyeing the position of Faye's bag. "But she's picked up the Tower's rhythm. She's starting to notice patterns."

Helena crouched beside the bench near the archway. She reached under it, pulled out a small folded card, and moved it three inches to the right. Then she stood, brushed off her hands.

"She'll find it now, when she sits. It'll anchor the memory."

"You're sure she won't feel the shift?"

Helena gave him a dry look. "She might. But it won't matter. People forgive the impossible when it makes them feel certain."

They returned to the sundial bench.

Helena released the glyph.

Time resumed.

Faye blinked. Her eyes fell on the bench. She moved toward it, sat, and—exactly as planned—noticed the folded card. She picked it up, read the front. Her posture changed. She smiled, faintly, and opened her notebook.

"That's the last correction for the week," Aurelian said, settling back.

"Unless Lyla crosses the library steps early again."

He sighed. "She probably will."

Later that evening, in the west wing study hall, Wynn leaned across a table toward Ariela.

"Does Helena ever feel... off to you?" she asked, her voice low.

Ariela didn't look up from her notes. "Off how?"

"I don't know. She's just always *there*, you know? Just when you're about to say something, or do something, or need something. And not in a normal way. In a... rehearsed way."

Ariela paused, then tapped her pencil once.

"Yeah," she said. "Aurelian, too. He asked me a question in class yesterday—one I was about to ask *him*. Same words.

Same order."

Wynn sat back, thoughtful.

Across the room, Helena and Aurelian sat in silence at the far table. Their books were open. Neither of them turned around.

By the next week, the rumours had names.

The Glide, they called it.

Students whispered that Helena and Aurelian didn't walk like the rest of them. They moved as if the world had already cleared their path. Like they had been here once before and were just hitting their marks. Like actors. Or ghosts.

Helena heard the name during lunch. She didn't flinch.

Aurelian just said, "They're catching on faster than expected."

Helena looked over the courtyard. Faye was sketching. Ariela was pacing the edge of the reflecting pool. Lyla sat alone under the yew tree.

> *"Let them,"* she said. *"Suspicion isn't the same as proof."*

She closed her notebook. Inside, half a page glowed faintly.

The next move was already in place.

The First Confrontation

Year 2002, First Melt, 9th day

Between the silence and the spark.

Near the East Greenhouse Steps, a morning chill lingered. Frost clung to drooping leaves.

Lyla's day started with a misplaced journal.

After frantic searching she found it beneath her bed—except she hadn't left it there. She *never* left it there. She was meticulous. She knew the placement of every book, every page. And the moment her fingers touched the worn leather cover, something twisted in her gut.

She opened it to the last marked page.

The ink had dried. Her handwriting. But the sentence wasn't hers.

| *"Stability is a fiction best maintained by familiarity."*

She didn't remember writing it. But she remembered *thinking* it.

That was worse.

She cornered Helena the next morning—near the steps of the east greenhouse, just as the bells finished their chime.

There were no students nearby. Only the rustling of ferns and the occasional bird overhead.

"Helena," Lyla called.

Helena turned. She looked like she always did—composed, faintly amused, waiting for something Lyla hadn't said yet.

Lyla stopped two paces short.

"You've been... interfering."

Helena didn't blink. "That's vague."

"My journal," Lyla said. "Someone went through it. Placed it somewhere I didn't leave it. There's a sentence in it I don't remember writing."

"You've had gaps before," Helena offered calmly.

"Not like this," Lyla snapped. "This wasn't sleepwalking. This was inserted. Someone took a thought I hadn't spoken and left it for me to read later."

A pause. Helena's expression didn't change.

"You think it was me?"

"I don't think. I *know*. And it's not just me. Wynn's noticing. Ariela feels it. You and Aurelian—you're too precise. Too rehearsed."

Helena stepped forward—not threatening, just closer.

"You're not wrong," she said.

That stopped Lyla.

Helena continued, voice lower now. "We're not manipulating you. Not *you*. But we are... guiding. Correcting course."

> *"That's not your decision to make."*
>
> *"It is if no one else is willing to carry the weight."*

Lyla stared at her. "So you *are* doing it."

Helena nodded once with grace.

Lyla's jaw clenched. "Then say it."

> *"What?"*
>
> *"Say what you are."*

Helena hesitated. The wind stirred the edge of Lyla's coat. A memory passed behind Helena's eyes—too fast to catch.

> *"Careful."*
>
> *"Prepared."*
>
> *"Necessary."*
>
> *"And dangerous," Lyla said. "You're building something you won't explain. You say it's to help. But you only help when it suits your plan."*

Another pause.

Helena tilted her head. "You think I'm dangerous?"

Helena smiled brightly, but then her face disappeared.

Across the courtyard, stood 10 steps away already, Helena had moved away in an instant.

In Lyla's ear however, she heard Helena's voice in the low growl of a soundless sigil.

You have no idea.

Lyla grimaced. And for the first time, she feared she'd already lost.

The Door They Don't Open

Year 2002, First Melt, 11th day, Late afternoon

The door remembered—and the pain it carries.

Outside, light rain was suspended in the air—like tears uncried.

Inside, in the northeast corridor—there was one door they always paused at.

One moment they never rushed.

Not because it's dangerous.

Not because it risks exposure.

But because it *hurts*. Every time.

The northeast corridor was quiet. Long stone arches, faintly gold with lichen. A soft rain patterned the windows, caught in the frozen stillness of the Spiral. Raindrops suspended mid-air, like ink in water. For them, the world was paused.

The girl inside was crying.

A fragile scream—the sound of someone who tried to hold too much for too long.

Helena's footsteps slowed.

Her crystal pulsed faintly at her collar. She checked the field —stable, self-contained. The miniature sun in her left pocket hummed with quiet radiance—a warmth felt through the layers of her coat. No drain. No ice. No entropy here.

Aurelian leant against the far wall. His arms crossed—his expression unreadable.

> *"She always cries here,"* he said.

Helena nodded. Her hand touching the doorframe. "But not for the same reasons."

> *"No, not always."*

They had been here before. Time doesn't loop. They cannot rewind. But the Spiral ran deep—and echoes carry.

There is only one world. One moment. And it moves outward like ripples in a still lake, folding the Spiral into every breath.

And here — in this echo — the girl breaks.

Helena didn't hesitate this time.

She reached into the Spiral, expanding the field with a practiced breath. A golden shimmer pulsed from her skin— slow, careful, gentle—touching the girl with a needle of light spreading across her cheek. No fracture. No resistance. A soft stillness—holding her steady in a space that doesn't hurt.

The sobbing slowed.

Inside the room, the girl was seated on the floor, arms wrapped around her knees, face buried. Helena crossed the threshold, treading carefully.

She crouched without a word.

When she spoke, it was soft.

> *"You are not broken," she said.*

The girl didn't look up. But something in her posture shifted. The kind of stillness that listens.

Helena set a slip of paper beside her. Three lines of ink in her own hand:

> *The world will not remember this moment.*
> *But you will.*
> *And it will carry you forward.*

She rose, crossed the room, and touched the far wall—a silent gesture of sealing, of containment. No trace left behind but the warmth.

Outside, Aurelian watched with sympathy.

> *"She won't know it was us," he said.*
> *"She doesn't need to."*

They let the field contract.

The golden shimmer withdrew. The girl returned to the flow of time like a leaf settling on still water—unaware, unharmed, but lighter somehow. She breathed in, rubbed her eyes, and rose up.

When the Spiral releases, the world exhales.

Rain resumed its fall. Downstairs the corridor stirred again.

Helena and Aurelian walked on.

The Candle

Year 2002, First Melt, 13th day – Flame against fatigue.

They activated the Spiral in an empty hallway. The first bell had not yet rung. Rain smudged the glass, frozen like ice. It was the kind of day that made people quiet.

Rain drifted through mist, soft and directionless, smudging the towers of the academy into distant shapes. The stone corridors were slick underfoot, and even the bravest spells burned a little duller in the gloom. Students moved slowly through the halls, coats buttoned high, eyes glassy from cold and sleeplessness. It was near the end of winter, and the weight of it was being felt in every corner of the building.

Sniffles were common. Sighs were frequent. Everyone was waiting for spring.

Before the bell, before the first muddy boots squeaked through the lecture wing, Helena and Aurelian stepped through the doorway in to an empty classroom. The Spiral, pulsing around them, held the world like breath between heartbeats.

Desks sat crooked in their rows. Chalk floated mid-air over a half-finished sigil. Outside the window, a raindrop hung just before hitting the sill, fat and perfect and motionless.

Neither of them spoke.

Helena walked to the front of the room, where a brass candlestick sat unused beside a pile of spellbooks. With a gloved hand, she sparked the wick. The flame caught on the first try, rising into a gentle flicker. Warmth spread from the small circle of light, faint but unmistakable.

Behind her, Aurelian stepped forward and caught her wrist lightly.

> *"Come now, Helena," he said, smiling just a little. "That's every room in the academy now."*

She said nothing, but her eyes stayed on the flame. It danced in the stillness finding its own sense of belonging— like it had always been waiting.

Moments later, the Spiral released. Time surged back into place with the soft rush of returning breath.

The bell rang.

The students arrived.

They filed in without fanfare, chattering softly, brushing water from sleeves and boots. One girl paused at the sight of the candle. She blinked, confused for a moment, then smiled. She didn't know why it was there. It just was. It felt like a kindness no one had to explain.

Later that evening, in the dormitories, a new gift appeared.

Each student found a small white box in their locker. Inside: a slice of cake, carefully wrapped and perfectly fresh. Beside it sat a folded note, written in looping, unmistakably human handwriting.

No two notes were the same.

Laughter bloomed in the common rooms. More than one person cried. Some tried to figure out the origin—who had baked, who had delivered, how such a feat had gone entirely unnoticed. But the bakers denied any involvement. The quartermaster reported no missing funds. There was no record, no signature, no answer.

There was the cake, and the notes, and the unmistakable feeling that they had been seen. That they had been remembered. That someone cared.

Aurelian stood by a window that overlooked the eastern wing, watching as a group of younger students passed beneath him with their boxes tucked under their arms like gifts from a dream.

"Why must we do this?" he asked.

Helena didn't look up from her journal. She was sitting cross-legged on the floor, scribbling something quickly before she forgot it.

"Because I wanted to see the smile," she said.

One more room waited.

Far across the academy, tucked away behind the northeast corridor—where no classes were scheduled and no students were meant to go—a single chair had been placed in the centre of a small, forgotten space.

On it sat a candle.

A slice of cake.

And a letter.

The candle was already lit.

The cake was still warm.

The letter was long, and written by hand. No spells. No illusions. Just ink and truth and care.

Eventually, a girl entered.

She looked around warily, as if expecting a trick. Her eyes were red. Her face was pale. She walked with her arms wrapped around herself like armour.

But the room was quiet. The candle burned clean. The chair had not moved.

She approached slowly, rubbing at her eyes with the back of her hand. When she saw the note, she hesitated—then read it. All of it. Twice.

She didn't eat the cake right away. She didn't sit, not at first. She just stood there, holding the letter in shaking fingers.

Eventually, she sat down beside the chair, not in it. Cross-legged. Grounded. Breathing.

She took out a pencil from her coat pocket and began to write in the margins. Quiet thoughts. A few lines of poetry. Something that might become a question. Or an answer.

The candle's heat dried her tears.

The sweetness cut through the numbness.

And the letter—the letter told her something she hadn't heard in far too long: that she mattered. That someone had seen her fall and left a light where she might land.

She folded the note carefully. Put it in her coat.

Clutched the candle in both hands.

Maybe tomorrow, she thought, just maybe—

tomorrow might be okay

after all.

A conversation remembered

Year 2002, First Melt, 16th day

When spring light returns, and memory hums like an old tune.

Faye sat on a courtyard bench between towers, watching the early spring breeze scattering blossoms. Her sketchbook open—pencil poised to capture the moment.

This wasn't planned. Of course not.

They hadn't written it in a ledger. Hadn't circled the date or planned their meeting like they once would have. It was just a bench. A soft spring wind. A courtyard between towers that had no name, only flowering trees with petals that collected in Faye's open sketchbook.

Wynn arrived with two cups of tea and a box of lemon biscuits, balanced precariously in the crook of her arm.

Faye didn't look up, but the corner of her mouth twitched.

> *"Late."*
>
> *"Only a little," Wynn said, sitting beside her with a dramatic exhale. "Besides, you started without me."*
>
> *"I'm just sketching light," Faye said. "It doesn't wait."*

Wynn looked at the page. Pale blossoms, the curve of the wall, three birds in midair.

> *"It never does," Wynn said softly, and handed her a cup.*

They sat in silence for a while. Tea steam curled around their fingers. A breeze carried petals across the stones like drifting pages.

Eventually, Wynn said, "Do you think they miss us?"

Faye didn't answer right away. She closed her sketchbook carefully, as though sealing something living inside.

> *"They remember," she said. "But memory is different than missing."*
>
> *"You think they've moved on?"*
>
> *"I think... they've continued. As they were meant to. Like we did."*

Wynn nodded. She took a biscuit, bit the edge, frowned dramatically. "Ugh. Crushed."

Faye smiled faintly. "You always forget the tin."

> *"I never forget the tin. I just forget to bring it."*

They laughed, and it didn't echo like the observatory. It didn't hum like the Spiral. But it *stayed* in the air, full and unweighted.

Wynn leaned back against the bench, arms draped lazily across the backrest. "You know," she said, "sometimes I wonder if we ever really *left.*"

Faye arched a brow. "We're not part of it anymore."

> *"Sure," Wynn said. "But also—what if they're still*
> *following us? Just not to track or trap or reset time.*
> *What if they just... want to know how we're doing?"*

Faye looked at her for a long moment. "You think time has feelings."

> *"I think we gave them some," Wynn said. "That*
> *counts."*

Another silence followed, softer this time.

Then, from Faye: "They gave me a place to leave my dreams."

> *"I know. You told me."*
> *"I still don't know how much of it I wrote."*
> *"Does it matter?"*

Faye thought for a moment. Then she shook her head. "No. Not anymore."

> *"I got a locket," Wynn said. She pulled it out from*
> *under her collar. "Want to hear the song again?"*

Faye nodded and Wynn opened the shell with a practiced flick. A tune filled the air—simple, lilting, and a little off-key.

Faye closed her eyes.

> *"I still don't remember the first time you sang it,"* she
> said.
>
> *"But you remember what it meant,"* Wynn whispered.

Faye opened her eyes and looked toward the sky.

> *"Yes,"* she said. *"I do."*

The notes played out.

When the silence returned, neither of them rushed to fill it.

Faye leaned her head on Wynn's shoulder. Wynn didn't
flinch. She leaned back, resting her cheek against Faye's
hair.

> *"You know,"* Wynn murmured, *"I don't think they
> made us forget."*
>
> *"No?"*
>
> *"I think they just trusted us to remember the right
> parts."*

Faye nodded. Her hand found Wynn's, warm against the
chill of spring stone.

And somewhere, not far at all—perhaps behind a wall, or
just beneath the skin of the world—a candle flickered.

A spiral turned. And two names were spoken in a breath
that wasn't quite air.

Chapter VIII — The Embrace

Year 2002, Breaking, 3rd day

All the time in the world, and still they must pretend.

"Helena?" called the professor from across the classroom. "I have your exam results here, a near perfect year. Well done."

Helena stood from her desk at the back of the airy room. Bright, summery light carried a fresh breeze through tall alcoves. She straightened the folds in her schooldress with a neat symmetrical push to the floor, and stepped carefully out to the side of the desks, striding forward to meet the professor at the front. She gave a slight curtsy at the front as she took the parchment; a stamped and sealed document, silver-trimmed on official academy paper, with the blue wax seal of the professor. A glyph nestled under the seal rotated slowly within the substrate of the paper; the official mark and magic of passing her first year at the academy. The class gave a quick applause, before moving on to the next student.

Aurelian stood just outside the room, with Faye, Wynn, and other second years congratulating their undergraduate friends.

After the mild-mannered ceremony the documents were scrolled away into smart paper tubes, tied with blue ribbons, and packed away in bags ready to be sent home to their parents for the summer break.

Out in the gardens, tea and refreshments had been provided, and the elder students played lively songs on an array of instruments. Not everyone had made it as far as graduation. A month before, the cut was made for the year. Almost one-fifth of the students who struggled the most with magic were sent home. Not with harshness, but something like safety. Recommendation letters in hand. These students would soon find apprenticeships elsewhere; their refined knowledge perfectly suited in the kingdom – but not at a level suitable to continue at the academy.

Aurelian and Helena had long considered interfering, but the academy's traditions had stood for centuries. The world outside this valley was at peace. The neighbouring countries traded freely, and the Kings, Queens, and democracies that surrounded them flourished. Those with magic knew how to defuse, to guide, to remind. Helena and Aurelian had grown up in a world where those instincts were natural.

Lost in thought, Lyla gave Helena a tap on her shoulder with her certificate roll. There was the tiniest of flickers as it landed on her shoulder. Lyla *noticed*. "Hey, Ms Helena? Day dreaming again?"

Helena sighed, her shoulders dropping deeply down to her sides, almost comically folding up on the chair. Turning her head to face Lyla, she gave a friendly smile. "It's such a relief; I feel like I've been here *forever.*"

That final forever seemed to linger in the air a little too loudly. Actually, Lyla wasn't even sure if Helena *had* spoken. The words just appeared somewhere near her head. "Actually," Helena continued, this time aloud, in a more normal voice "I'm glad to have made it this far. Few even dream of making it to the school, let alone to the end of their first year."

"We all have bright futures," retorted Lyla, "You know we're the best of the bunch."

Something in Helena's eye twinkled. Her saggy demeanour tightening with the merest of frustration. Not from anger. Restlessness. She pushed herself back on the seat with her arms straightened, gave a methodical kick of her legs in the faintest mock tantrum, and growled. "Garhhhhhg. Why do I have to do this dance!", still kicking herself back upright.

> *"Dance?" queried Lyla, somewhat bemused, watching her friend right herself back into a graceful sitting position.*
>
> *"All of this"—Helena waved—"all this serenity, the jokes, the games, the drama."*

> *"We're just kids. We deserve time to grow. It can't all be work and no play."*

Lyla sipped her tea.

> *"Besides, it's important to celebrate just as much as it is to dream."*

Helena grumpily agreed with a nod, lazily reaching out with a fresh slump of her arm for a biscuit.

> *"What has ever got into you today?"*

Lyla pushed the tray of biscuits closer for Helena to reach.

> *"It's the relief I guess. No more pressure. All the time in the world."*

Lyla distracted for a moment, perked up with a thought.

> *"You're visiting right? My house for summer? I made sure to invite the both of you."*

Helena looked up from the table, her chin resting low, a biscuit inches from her hand.

> *"Of course. Wouldn't miss it for the world,"* rolling her eyes at the thought.

Lyla could see something else was at play in Helena's private bubble of time.

"I know you wouldn't," replied Lyla, sipping her tea, her back straight with grace and confidence.

Aurelian decided an "are you feeling alright?" wasn't quite the mood to strike with Helena today. They'd both agreed to limit use of the necklaces for a short while. Helena had been up late preparing her clothes, packing her bags, generally being distant. It was so easy to regress into their old forms. The life at the academy had a certain rhythm. Their young bodies still prone to tiredness, sickness, injury. They still had to age, despite living lifetimes between moments, there was a toll to be paid in the "real" world. To preserve appearances for school, and their families, they had normal lives to lead. However, to escape fully from their mortality, they would first have to live those lives. The device, the spiral, would always be in arms reach. The power to freeze time, or more technically, dilate time around them. Time to do anything, to do *everything*. To go anywhere, and come back again. But they still had to live. Still talk to their classmates. Still write reports for teachers. Still eat breakfast, and dinners. Stress rose and fell inside Helena. Endless opportunities. Limited time. Endless time. Knowledge compounded. She needed an *out*.

Out in the gardens, the breeze had grown warmer, coaxing the late blooms into motion. Helena sat with her certificate tucked neatly under her tea saucer. A bee circled her biscuit and was gently waved away without looking. Lyla had wandered off to join the music.

Aurelian approached, a cup in one hand and a folded paper in the other.

> *"You left this in the hallway," he said, offering the note.*
>
> *"I know. I wanted to see if you'd notice."*
>
> *"You're getting careless," he said. "Or you're leaving trails."*

She shrugged, and accepted both the paper and the tea without meeting his gaze.

> *"Sometimes I forget who I'm pretending to be."*

Later, after the celebration had thinned into twilight, Aurelian found her again—beneath the twisted copper yew, where lanterns glowed and steam from the kitchen vents painted the stone soft with warmth.

They didn't speak. He sat beside her and handed her a book she hadn't seen since their third Spiral.

> *"From the vault," he said. "The binding's reset. I thought you could do with some reassurance."*
>
> *"I remember," she replied, tracing the cracked leather with reverent fingers.*
>
> *"That's why I brought it."*

The following morning, Helena stood alone in the east corridor, watching students bustle past with luggage and plans. A boy brushed her shoulder, muttered an apology, and didn't notice the flicker of stillness that passed over her skin.

She smiled, then stepped into the breakfast hall.

Everything was already ready.

Aurelian sat at their usual table. The toast was warm. The butter soft. The tea steaming. The paper folded into precise quarters, as if the morning had been waiting just for them.

> *"You cheated," he said.*
>
> *"I arranged," she replied, buttering a crumpet with serene precision.*

In the lecture hall, the morning's guest professor fumbled a quote on Chrono-Spatial Refraction. The class moved on. But Helena winced.

Aurelian caught her eye from across the room and gave a tiny shake of his head: don't.

She didn't.

That night, they walked the still Spiral back to the hall, passing frozen dust motes in mid-float. Helena bent beneath the old lectern and carved the correction gently into the underside with a shard of starlight chalk.

> *"The truth should always be somewhere," she murmured.*
>
> *"Even if it's hidden," Aurelian replied.*

Faye caught Helena humming.

> *"That's familiar," Faye said.*

Helena blinked, lips still parted, sound now absent.

> *"You taught it to me," Faye added, smiling.*
>
> *"Of course," Helena said lightly. "It's an old tune."*

But later that evening, she quietly filed a note under her pillow. The page was headed: Spiral Leakage — Archive B. Beneath it: "No humming. No slipping. Memory harmonics increasing."

A letter arrived from home.

Handwritten, brown-edged from travel, smelling faintly of hearth ash and dried pears. Helena opened it slowly, the way one opens the past when unsure whether it still belongs.

> *"We miss you, darling. Your father says the stars are bright over the orchard again. I think of you every time I smell rain on lavender."*

She folded the letter gently and slid it under her mattress without a reply. She had already lived a year since she'd read the last one.

Before the term ended, they spiralled one final time—no reason, no mission, no need. Just a moment.

A clearing behind the west tower. Low grass. A single lantern still burning.

They lay back, limbs brushing, eyes skyward.

> *"We could stay," Aurelian said softly.*
>
> *"We won't," Helena replied. "But we could."*

Their crystals pulsed once in unison, dim and content. The Spiral hummed around them, unasked and unquestioned.

They watched the stars blink into stillness. Listened to the world hold its breath. Then let it go again.

| **Departure** |

Year 2002, Breaking, 4th day – A train to catch.

The last day of term arrived. Students flooded the rail platform with trunks and laughter, some crying, others sprinting to catch the final carriages. The world moved on.

Helena stood by the fountain, coat fastened, bag neatly packed. Aurelian joined her, his satchel slung effortlessly, looking for all the world like a boy about to spend the summer with friends.

> *"Did you bring the vault?" she asked.*
>
> *"Already packed."*
>
> *"And the index?"*
>
> *"All safe—encrypted—hidden away."*
>
> *"Amazing."*

They turned in step and walked toward the coaches, pausing only once—beside the eastern yew.

A girl sat alone beneath it, cross-legged, sketching the roots. Her eyes lifted briefly to Helena's as they passed. A flicker. A hand resting on a cheek.

The girl held the new warmth to her face.

Aboard the train, as they settled into their compartment—coats shed and bags stowed overhead—Helena stretched out her legs and leaned against the window.

Aurelian fiddled with the lock, trying to line up the latch with a damaged faceplate.

> *"We're not the same," she said.*
>
> *"We're not meant to be," Aurelian replied.*
>
> *"And yet here we are. Still taking trains. Still sipping tea. Still pretending to be..."*
>
> *"Us?"*

Helena laughed quietly.

> *"Well us, do you think they'll be ready when we arrive?"*
>
> *He shrugged. "That's the joy of finding out."*

Sitting down beside Helena, he removed a slim notebook and pen from his coat, cracked the spine, and turned to the first blank page. Glistening ink shimmered faintly from the tip. She pressed closer, embracing his arm to take a closer look.

At the top of the page, in Helena's handwriting, was a one word title, underlined twice for emphasis:

Ascension

Folio

This artbook belongs to Faye.

If found please return to the 3rd year dorm in the west tower.

Helena

"Helena is always thinking, and always forgetting to eat. I hope she never loses her sense of wonder, or her keen insight. She always made me feel like the brightest star in the room."

Aurelian

"Aurelian, sweet, quiet, reserved Aurelian. Part watcher, part mentor. Always patient, never rushed. He always drew me closer, even as I sketched."

Wynn

"Whimsical wynn. Bubbly, wonderful, kind. Never afraid to show her emotions. Forever collecting trinkets and stories. And memories, always treasured memories. "

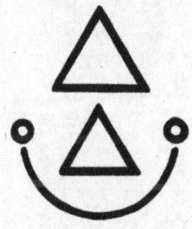

Lyla

"Lovely Lyla. Intelligent, precocious, one step ahead of us. Beautiful in her own way, but never cruel. Destined for greatness I'm sure."

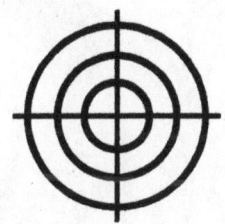

Ariela

"Ariela is charming from the first moment to the last. Told me exactly where to find the best light. Keen sense of story and space. Helped me find my voice when maybe I was lost in thought."

Faye (Self Portrait)

"Me! Shy perhaps? Quiet confidence. Joyous. Observant. These portraits are for you, my dearest friends; because someone had to draw the silence between the moments."

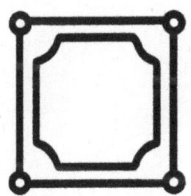

Thanks for reading.

Visit jmarkavian.com for digital editions and more.